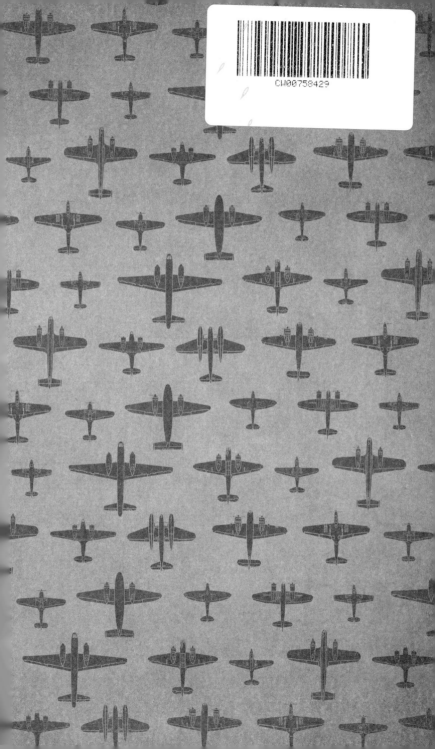

Biggles Sees It Through

William Earl Johns was an English adventure writer, best known as the creator of the beloved Biggles stories, which drew on his experience as a pilot in the First World War. After his flying career with the RAF, Johns became a newspaper air correspondent, an occupation he combined with editing and illustrating books about flying. He wrote over 160 books, including nearly 100 Biggles titles.

Also by Captain W. E. Johns and published by Canelo

BIGGLES
SEES IT
THROUGH

CAPT·W·E·JOHNS

CANELO

First published in the United Kingdom in 1941 by Oxford University Press

This edition published in the United Kingdom in 2022 by

Canelo
Unit 9, 5th Floor
Cargo Works, 1-2 Hatfields
London, SE1 9PG
United Kingdom

A CIP catalogue record for this book is available from the British Library.

Print ISBN 978 1 80436 061 3
Ebook ISBN 978 1 80032 911 9

Look for more great books at www.canelo.co

Printed and bound in Great Britain by Clays Ltd, Elcograf S.p.A.

I

MIX
Paper from
responsible sources
FSC
www.fsc.org
FSC® C018072

Introduction

The Biggles books were some of the first I ever read, holding a special place in my heart, as they do for so many readers the world over.

I was transfixed by Biggles, Algy and Ginger's daring dogfights with the Germans in the World Wars, their secretive actions behind enemy lines under the nose of the nefarious Erich von Stalhein, and their adventures to far-flung corners of the globe in search of lost gold or missing friends. And, no matter where Biggles & Co. went, they took with them an unfailing and irrepressible sense of adventure, heroism and the calm certainty that they were fighting for something bigger than themselves, often with an almost casual disregard for the danger they were putting themselves in.

Captain William Earl Johns and I share a professional association: he as a pilot in the Royal Flying Corps in WWI, me as a Tornado navigator in the Royal Air Force. While propellers had been replaced by jet engines when I took to the skies, the freedom of flight, of being up there above the clouds, is something that all aviators know and love. And it is this freedom that typifies so many of Biggles's adventures when airborne travel, navigation and reconnaissance were a relatively new concept.

The stories span the globe, letting readers imagine faraway lands and the dangers they held from the safety of their favourite reading spot. In response to some summons or crisis, Biggles would often hop into his aircraft and fly to Belize, Borneo, or northern Canada, completing journeys in hours that would have taken days or weeks by other means, tackling problems – and villains – in this new frontier: the sky.

That imagination was further fired by Johns's passionate descriptions of the aircraft themselves. Whether it was a Sopwith Camel, the trusty Spitfire, a Bristol Blenheim or a Beaufighter, to read Biggles was to get caught up in the characters's love of flying machines. It is still possible to see some of those early aircraft at airshows today, where the famous drone of their engines provides a glorious soundtrack that echoes from the pages of these stories.

But why do the stories still hold such a strong appeal for readers, both new and returning?

For me, it is because the Biggles stories hark back to a simpler time now lost to us, before telecommunications, social media and the internet dominated our lives, when aerial combat was a duel of skill and chance in the skies. Biggles's aircraft didn't bristle with the mind-boggling array of electronic countermeasures, radar and laser-guided munitions of the Tornados I flew. For him, it was just his engine, and the stick and pedals that controlled the machine in a beautiful mechanical symbiosis.

It is also Biggles's courage and ability to improvise in the face of adversity – not to mention the bravery of his team, whom he had to trust with his life – that keeps readers coming back. Biggles, Algy and Ginger conducted daring adventures with a sense of decency, positivity and honour, and expected the same code of ethics from their allies and enemies alike, as can be seen in their numerous run-ins with von Stalhein!

Combine this unfettered passion and these incredible characters with Johns's seemingly inexhaustible supply of adventures (he wrote almost 100 Biggles tales), and you have a perfect recipe for a series that pulls the reader back, and leaves a lasting impression of the hero. Perhaps a hero we would all like to see in ourselves?

These new hardback editions from Canelo capture the essence of the Biggles books, with wonderful new covers featuring the very aircraft that appear in the novel in operation. They are also editions to be treasured, easily taking pride of place on the shelf of any Biggles fan, old or new.

I wish you many happy hours reading them.

John Nichol
Sunday Times bestselling author of *Spitfire*, *Lancaster* and *Tornado*
www.johnnichol.com
Hertfordshire, March 2022

Biggles Sees It Through

CHAPTER I

An Eventful Reconnaissance

From twenty thousand feet Squadron-Leader James Bigglesworth, D.S.O., better known to his friends as 'Biggles', looked down upon a world that revealed no more signs of occupation than the moon. From time to time his eyes, whimsical and faintly humorous, switched to the atmosphere around him, and then settled for a moment on the bewildering array of dials that smothered his instrument board. His eyes ran over them swiftly, for years of experience enabled him to read them as easily as a schoolmaster reads a book. Once in a while he glanced at his companion sitting in the second pilot's seat, Flight-Lieutenant the Hon. Algernon Lacey, D.F.C., and, still more rarely, behind him at the slim, watchful figure of Flying-Officer 'Ginger' Hebblethwaite, manning the centre gun-turret of the Bristol Blenheim. The fourth occupant of the aircraft, Flight-Sergeant Smyth, master mechanic, he could not see, for he was squatting humped up over a gun in the tail.

For nearly four hours these positions had been maintained with practically no variation, each airman concentrating on his particular task to the exclusion of all else, knowing full well the penalty of relaxation in the most deadly form of warfare devised by human ingenuity

I

– war flying, wherein mercy is never expected and rarely encountered. During the whole of the four hours nothing had happened; the engines roared, the propellers slashed their way through air that was frozen into immobility, the instrument needles quivered. Far to the north the rim of the sun, a slip of glowing crimson, just showed above a jagged horizon that was the Arctic Circle, and shed an eerie twilight on a world of ice-bound desolation.

So this, thought Ginger, surveying the frozen panorama from his glass-protected turret, was Finland. He had been eager enough to go with the others when the Air Ministry had allowed Biggles to accompany a party of volunteers to help the Finns in their struggle against Soviet aggression, but now that he was there he saw no reason to congratulate himself. They had been in Finland only a week, but as far as he was concerned it was enough. Practically forbidden to fly over Russian territory, their work had been confined to long-distance reconnaissance raids along the frontiers, and since they encountered little opposition – and there was nothing to see on the ground except snow – it was becoming monotonous. Presently they would return to their base at Oskar, where they would have to spend an hour swathing the machine in rugs to prevent the oil from freezing. Tomorrow there would be another uneventful reconnaissance. Yes, it was becoming monotonous. He yawned.

At the same moment Biggles's voice came from the internal communication transmitter at his elbow.

'Enemy aircraft on the starboard quarter. Stand by to attack.'

Simultaneously with the words the Blenheim banked and dived steeply for speed.

Faintly above the roar of the racing engines came Biggles's voice, singing: 'Roll out the barrel...'

As he swung his turret to face the field of attack, Ginger's lips pursed up to echo the catchy tune. He saw the enemy aircraft at once, a Polycarpov bomber, one of the type being used by the Russians for the bombing of Finnish towns. It was also diving – for home, proving that the pilot had seen them.

Biggles's lips parted in a smile, for he knew that he had the 'legs' of the Russian.

Steeper and steeper became the Russian's dive as he sought escape in sheer speed, but steeper, too, became the dive of the Blenheim.

Ginger aligned his gun, bracing himself against the terrific drag of centrifugal force, and waited. The Russian seemed to swim towards them, sideways. But still he waited. The distance between the two machines closed; the Russian was no longer misty grey, but clear and dark. Jabs of orange flame showed where the Russian gunners were already firing.

Straight under the enemy machine Biggles dived, and then rocketed upwards, and the Blenheim vibrated slightly as its guns began to stutter.

The front gun having fired its burst, the Blenheim turned slowly, giving Ginger and Smyth in the rear seat their chance. Both took it: their guns roared as one.

The dive of the Soviet bomber steepened for a moment, then its nose jerked upwards. Ginger gave it another burst – he was very close now. Smyth's gun took up the staccato chatter, and a stream of bullets played a vicious tattoo on the Russian's cockpit. It dropped a wing and fell sideways into a spin. The fight was over.

Biggles brought the Blenheim to an even keel and watched the Russian go down, ready to renew the attack should the spin turn out to be only a trick; but it was no sham. Black, oily smoke began to pour from its side; the cantilever wing broke across the middle, and the fuselage plunged earthward like a huge torpedo. It seemed to go on falling for a long time, long after it looked as if it must have reached the ground. But the end came at last. Clouds of snow mingled with the black smoke as it struck the frozen earth and spread itself in a thousand splinters over an acre of ground.

Biggles glanced at Algy, and for a moment their eyes met. Both faces were expressionless, for they had seen the same thing happen too many times to be upset by the dreadful spectacle. It was an unpleasant but inevitable part of air fighting.

Humming quietly, Biggles turned away and began to climb for height, but his eyes were on the ground, making a hasty reconnaissance while they were so close to it. Suddenly his tune broke off short and his body stiffened, his eyes focused on a speck that moved slowly across a flat sheet of ice which he knew to be the frozen surface of one of the hundreds of lakes that form a major part of the Finnish landscape. On one side of it a ridge of black rock projected through the snow like a crocodile's back; near it was a small dark object that seemed to stagger, fall, and then stagger on again, only to fall once more.

Biggles spoke tersely. 'What d'you make of it?'

'It's a man,' returned Algy briefly, his eyes on the object.

'That's what I thought.'

The Blenheim's engines faded into a moan that was like the death-cry of a dying giant, and the machine sank earthward. The wind sighed over wings and fuselage.

At a height of a hundred feet Biggles circled the man on the ground, now lying where he had last fallen.

'He's all in, whoever he is,' remarked Algy.

Biggles made a swift survey of the lake's icy surface.

Algy guessed what was in his mind. 'Are you thinking of going down?'

'I don't like it, but I think we must. We can't leave the poor blighter to die.'

'It seems silly to risk four lives to save one – particularly when ten thousand men are dying every day along the Mannerheim Line.'

'I agree, but this isn't quite the same thing. If I don't try to save him, the thought of that poor wretch lying out here in the snow will spoil my sleep tonight. It'll spoil yours, too, so don't kid yourself.'

'All right – go ahead.'

'Stand by to land,' called Biggles into the microphone to warn the gunners of his intention.

He brought the machine down very carefully, his hand on the throttle ready to zoom again the moment an obstacle showed itself. But there was none; the surface of the frozen lake was like powdered glass, and the Blenheim ran to a smooth standstill some thirty yards from where the motionless form was lying.

Biggles studied the sky carefully in all directions before he would allow anyone to get out; then he slipped his emergency brandy flask into his pocket, climbed down, and with Algy and Ginger following, walked quickly towards the body. Over everything hung the silence of death. Nothing moved.

Biggles was first to reach the unknown man, who, it was now seen, was old and grey. He dropped on his knees, and lifting up the limp head, stared down into a face that

5

was pinched with cold and thin from suffering. The eyes were open. Unscrewing the top of his spirit flask with his teeth, he coaxed a little of the brandy between the blue lips. The man coughed instantly as the fiery liquid stung his throat; its effect was instantaneous and he struggled into a sitting position, muttering something in a language that none of them understood.

Biggles had picked up a few words of Finnish since he had been in the country, and he tried them, but they appeared to convey nothing. He tried French, but the man only shook his head. Finally, in desperation, he tried English. 'Who are you?' he said.

To his amazement the man answered in the same language.

'Are you – English?' he said.

Biggles replied, 'Yes, we're English. Who are you, and what are you doing here? But perhaps you'd better not try to talk yet; we'll carry you to our plane and get you somewhere safe.'

The old man shook his head. 'No,' he breathed with difficulty. 'It's – too late.'

'Too late? Surely not.'

'You don't understand. I am wounded – by – a bullet. What I have to say I must say now, or it will be – too late – and it is – important.'

'We'll get you into the machine, anyway,' declared Biggles.

'No – I implore you. When I die you must leave me here.'

Biggles stared.

'If you take me somewhere – I may be – recognised – by a spy, and then it would be known – that I had

– escaped. It would be better if it were thought that I had died – without speaking.'

Biggles looked nonplussed, but he nodded. 'Very well,' he said. 'I gather there is something you want to tell me. Here, have some more brandy; it may help you.'

The old man drank the spirit gratefully, and it brought a faint flush into his sunken cheeks. 'Yes; listen carefully,' he said. 'I am a Pole. I was a scientist working for the government in Warsaw. When the Germans marched into Poland I was on the point of concluding important experiments with metal alloys for aircraft – experiments that might well revolutionise the whole business of metal aircraft construction. Rather than destroy the fruits of seven years of labour, I put all my papers in a portfolio, and sought to escape so that I could give them to the Allies. But then it was hard to get out of my unhappy Poland. To make matters more difficult, the Germans knew all about me and my work, and when they found that I had gone they pursued me; they hunted for me everywhere. All frontiers were closed. There was only one way I could get out – by air. Our pilots were flying to neutral countries to save their machines. I found one willing to help me, and we fled to Russia, only to find that the Russians, too, had marched against us. We had only a little petrol left, so we tried to get to Finland. But the German Secret Service learned of my escape by aeroplane and traced it to Russia; they knew the number of the machine, and we had no means of painting it over. German pursuit planes flew over Russia to catch us, and they were close enough to shoot at us when we flew into a blizzard near Lake Ladoga. I had been hit by a bullet, and, although I did not know it, so had my pilot; but he flew on until the petrol gave out. Where we came down I don't know, for we had been lost in the blizzard, but we crashed into the side of a frozen lake, which must be one of the smaller lakes near Lake Ladoga.'

'In Finland or in Russia?' put in Biggles quickly.

'I'm not sure – Finland, I hope. But let me finish. My brave pilot died there. I knew that the German and Russian planes would still be looking for us, so rather than risk the papers falling into their hands, I hid the portfolio under some rocks near the wrecked plane. Then I started walking westward, hoping to meet some friendly Finns. But I saw no one. I had no food. It began to snow. I have been walking for three days, I think – I don't know how long. Give me – brandy.'

Biggles saw that the old man was near the end, for the shadow of death had already settled on his pale face. There was nothing more he could do except try to prolong the old man's life for a little while with the brandy.

'What is your name, sir? We ought to know,' he asked.

'Petolski. England knows of me. You must get the papers, but you must be quick or the Russians or the Germans will find them.'

'Can you give me any clearer directions for finding them?'

'They are about fifty paces east of the broken plane, under a large rock.'

'And how far is the lake from here?'

'Twenty – thirty – perhaps forty miles. I don't know. I may have – wandered. Tell – tell—' The old man's head had begun to droop. A shadow had crossed his eyes, which were staring unseeingly into the sky.

Biggles moved the flask nearer to the lips, but stopped suddenly as the body went limp in his arms. 'He's gone

– poor old fellow,' he said quietly, and allowed the body to sink slowly to the snow-covered ice.

'What are we going to do with him?' inquired Algy. 'I know he said we were to abandon him, but I hate the idea of just leaving the poor old chap lying here—' He broke off short as a yell came from Smyth.

The three airmen sprang to their feet. Simultaneously they heard the roar of an aero engine suddenly switched on. One glance was enough. Flying low, racing towards the spot, was an aeroplane, a German Messerschmitt.

'Quick!' snapped Biggles. 'Get aboard!' He dashed to the Blenheim.

Had the Messerschmitt pilot been a little less impetuous, or had he been a better shot, the affair might well have ended there and then, for he got in his first burst while the Blenheim was still on the ground. True, Biggles, realising his danger, jerked the throttle wide open, and the instant the machine began to move he jammed on one wheel brake, producing a skid so violent that Smyth, sitting in the tail, was nearly sick. Before the Messerschmitt could turn and fire again Biggles had his machine in the air, following the German and keeping underneath him, thus rendering his deadly front guns ineffective, although from this position Ginger had a clear view of the sleek fuselage. It may be that some of his shots took effect, for the Messerschmitt swerved away. Biggles seized the opportunity to bank steeply in the opposite direction, so that in a few seconds the two machines were a mile apart. He knew his business too well to fool about with a machine of higher manoeuvrability so far from home.

Keeping the stick forward, he tore westward with his wheels only a few feet from the ground, a position calculated to hamper the German pilot should he resume the attack, in that his speed would be chopped for fear of overshooting his mark and hitting the ground. The Messerschmitt did, in fact, chase the Blenheim for a little while, but it did not press the pursuit home, and when the German pilot suddenly turned back on his course Biggles guessed the reason: he had spotted the lonely figure on the ground.

Biggles actually turned the Blenheim, hoping to catch the Messerschmitt at rest on the lake as he himself had nearly been caught, but his ever watchful eyes picked out several other specks in the sky coming from the Russian frontier and he decided to let well alone. He pulled his nose round again to the west and headed for Oskar, which he reached some time later without further incident.

Leaving the others to attend to the machine, he borrowed a car and went straight down to Helsinki, no great distance away, where he reported to the British Consulate, feeling that the information he now possessed was too valuable to be lost.

It was nearly dark when he got back to Oskar, where he found the others congregated round the stove in the general mess, for the aerodrome was used by several units of the Finnish Air Force beside the International Squadron. However, he took them on one side and gave them the result of his mission.

'The Consul rang up London,' he said quietly. 'Ten minutes later Intelligence came through and I spoke to Colonel Raymond. It seems that our people know all about Petolski and his researches, so I wasn't surprised when Raymond asked me to try to get hold of the portfolio. He seemed mighty anxious about it, too. We've got to spare no effort to get those papers. If we can't get them ourselves we must at all costs prevent Germany getting hold of them.'

'How?' inquired Algy naively.

'How the deuce do I know!' returned Biggles. 'If we get them ourselves the Boche *can't* get 'em.'

'The Boche know about these papers?'

'Yes, Petolski told us so himself.'

'Then we look like having a lovely time playing hide and seek in the snow with a bunch of Huns.'

'I shouldn't be surprised at that,' admitted Biggles. 'Pity that confounded Messerschmitt came along. We can reckon that they found Petolski's body.'

'Which means that since they knew he escaped by air, they'll be looking for his crashed plane, hoping the papers will still be in it.'

Biggles nodded. 'We've got to get to it first.'

'When do we start?'

'At dawn. It's no use sitting here thinking about it; that won't get us anywhere. We may not come back.'

'You're telling me!' sneered Algy.

'What I meant was, not immediately. We'll take enough grub to last for two or three days, and some spare cans of petrol. I'll make a list of other things that might come in handy – things like skates.'

Algy started. 'Skates! Say, what *is* this – winter-sports?'

Biggles smiled. 'You've said it, laddie. Incidentally, it wouldn't be a bad idea if we took some white sheets to wrap ourselves in, for camouflage, as the Finns do.'

'Ha! Corpses on skates,' gibed Algy. 'I don't know what war's coming to.'

'You'll find out,' Biggles grinned.

'Why not paint the tops of our planes white, so that if any Huns come along they won't be so likely to spot us?' suggested Ginger.

'That's an idea,' agreed Biggles. 'I'll get the fellows onto it right away.'

'How about some snow-shoes, some skis, and a sledge or two?' suggested Algy sarcastically.

'Don't be a fool. This is no laughing matter – as you may discover if we run out of petrol and have to start walking.'

'I always did hate walking – you don't seem to get any place,' muttered Algy disgustedly.

'I'm not so keen on hiking myself,' admitted Biggles.

'You get your feet wet.'

'Absolutely. Ah, well, it may not come to that. Let's turn in; we may as well start fresh,' advised Biggles.

CHAPTER II

Ginger Makes a Discovery

The stars were paling in the sky the following morning when the Blenheim took off from the bleak aerodrome on its dangerous quest. Algy still persisted in adopting a facetious attitude about the whole thing, but he knew well enough the hazardous nature of the enterprise. Biggles had, of course, taken the Station Commander into his confidence to account for their temporary absence, for the supposed site of the crashed Polish machine was nearly three hundred miles from their base at Oskar, and since snow had fallen recently he suspected that it was going to be hard to spot the wreck from the air. But what concerned him most was the probability of running into hostile aircraft on the same mission as themselves, for while he had no fear that they would not be able to hold their own if it came to combat, too frequent encounters would not only diminish their petrol supply, but would seriously interfere with their search.

He flew in a straight line towards a point some distance north of Lake Ladoga, his objective being the area due east of where they had found the dying professor. This was actually about twenty miles inside the Finnish border, but the old man had been so hazy as to his whereabouts that it seemed just as likely that the crash would be in Russia as in Finland.

Reaching the spot, he started to circle, exploring with his eyes the many lakes over which the Blenheim passed; but it was obvious from the start that the search was not going to be easy. Owing to the snow it was difficult to see what was frozen water and what was snow-covered land. In the case of large lakes, the flat surface was, of course, a pretty good guide, but even so it was not easy to see where the water ended and the land began. Many times Biggles brought the machine nearly to the ground in order to make a closer examination of rocks that occasionally formed the shores of the lakes.

'I don't think it's any good going on like this,' he told Algy at last. 'We might go on doing this sort of thing for weeks without spotting the crash. Apart from the spare juice in the cans we're carrying, we've only just enough left to get home. We're over Russia now, anyway.'

'What are you going to do about it?'

'Land. We shall have to start working these lakes systematically − at any rate, the big ones. We'll land as near the bank as we dare and then explore on foot. If we draw blank we'll hop on to the next lake.'

Algy shook his head sadly. 'Seems a crazy business to me.'

'Can you think of anything better?'

'No.'

'Then don't be so infernally pessimistic. There is this about going down: the machine won't be so likely to be seen if we run into a bunch of Russians or Boche. Look at that.' The sun had just broken through the mist, and he pointed at the shadow of the Blenheim, huge and distorted, as black as pitch against the white background of snow, as it raced along below them. 'That shadow can be seen for miles,' he added.

Algy touched him on the arm. 'Take a look,' he said, pointing ahead.

Peering through the windscreen, Biggles saw five black specks against the sky high overhead; they were in arrow formation, and were obviously Messerschmitts. Instantly he cut the throttle and glided down, and the shadow on the ground seemed to come to meet the machine. As the wheels touched the surface of the frozen lake, machine and shadow came together and ran on to a stop.

'We'll sit here for a bit and hope they don't spot us,' said Biggles. 'I can't look for a crash and fight five Messers at the same time. I'm not a perishing magician.' He switched off and the propellers hissed viciously to a standstill. In the silence that followed the drone of the machines overhead sounded like the buzzing of angry hornets.

They watched them for some time without speaking. Then, 'They're going over,' said Algy. 'What do we do next?'

'I think we'll taxi over to those rocks,' returned Biggles, nodding towards a mass of black basalt that erupted out of the snow on the edge of the lake. 'Then we'll have a look at the map and start checking off the lakes one by one.'

'Okay,' agreed Algy.

Biggles took the machine to the spot he had indicated and then called the other two members of the crew forward. 'Well, here we are,' he said. 'We shall have to do a bit of exploring on foot. Smyth, you'll stay with the machine – keep your eyes skinned. Algy, you and Ginger go one way; I'll go the other; we'll meet at the far side, and if we don't find anything we'll come straight back and hop on to the next lake. Put a white sheet over your shoulders in case those Messers come back.'

They found nothing on the edge of that lake; nor did they find anything at the next, or the next, or the one after that. By mid-afternoon they were weary, and all they had done was to put a number of strokes on the map, indicating the lakes that had been searched.

'If we're going back we'd better start,' opined Algy.

'We're not going back,' returned Biggles, glancing at the sky. 'The weather looks settled so we may as well stay where we are.'

'And sleep in the machine?'

'Unless you prefer the snow,' smiled Biggles.

'To the deuce with that. I'm no Eskimo.'

'I suggest that we have a bite to eat, a few hours' rest, and then go on with the job,' put in Ginger. 'The sky is clear so it won't get dark.'

'That's true,' agreed Biggles. So far north, at that season of the year, it would not get really dark, as it would do farther south.

They made a satisfying but not particularly appetising meal from the stores they had brought with them, after which they lay down in the roomy fuselage to rest.

Ginger, however, could not sleep. Try as he would he could not get comfortable, with the result that he was soon in that unhappy state when he knew that, so far from sleeping, he was getting wider awake. The cold was intense, too, and the silence trying to the nerves. He knew that there was only one thing to do to break the spell, and that was to get up and have a walk round. Very quietly, therefore, he opened the door and stepped down into a twilit world so utterly devoid of life that he shivered. Buffing his arms, he walked up and down for a little while regarding the lonely landscape, wondering, naturally, about the quest on which they were engaged and if they would be successful.

Near at hand, where the ice-surfaced lake met the land, the ground rose steeply to a ridge. He did not know what lay beyond it, and the thought occurred to him to find out. Possibly there was another lake, in which case there was just a chance that it might turn out to be the one they were looking for; and it was really in the hope of finding a speedy solution to their problem that he made his way to the top of the ridge.

Before him stretched a panorama so awe-inspiring in its utter desolation that for a minute or two he stared at it aghast. Seen thus it looked much worse than it had done from the air. Snow covered everything, even the drooping firs that here and there clung to the stark hillsides.

He was about to turn away when a movement caught his eye, and looking round again quickly he saw that it was a flicker of light. At first he supposed it to be the aurora borealis, but soon dismissed this thought, for he perceived that it was much too low down, and of a warm yellow tint. It appeared to come from behind the next ridge, about a mile away, and as he stood staring he thought he heard a faint sound. Seized by curiosity, he at once determined to investigate. He glanced at the machine, but apparently the others were still sleeping, so without further delay he set off across the snow in the direction of the light.

Before he reached the ridge he had a pretty shrewd idea of what he would see on the other side, for the flicker of yellow light was now much brighter, and it could only mean one thing. Beyond the ridge a fire was burning, and a fire indicated the presence of human beings. Even so he was hardly prepared for the sight that met his startled gaze when, on hands and knees, he topped the rise and looked over.

He found himself staring down into a wide, flat depression, which he knew from experience, was another of the numerous lakes with which the district abounded. On the near side of it was a camp of six tents, arranged in a circle round a brightly burning fire, near which also a number of men were congregated. They were only about a hundred yards from where he lay. Faint snatches of conversation reached his ears, and although he could not speak Russian, he recognised the sounds of that language. Ginger noted a line of sledges, six in all, close by the tents. Six tents suggested that there were not less than thirty or forty men in the party, and it shocked him to think that they had been so close to danger without being aware of it. Clearly, Biggles would have to know about this at once.

He was about to turn away when a sound reached his ears that for a moment threw his brain into a whirl. It was the soft hum of wind over the fabric of a gliding aeroplane. The Russians evidently heard it too, for there was a sharp cry and more fuel was thrown on the fire, causing the flames to leap high; all of which suggested at once that the men were desirous of attracting the attention of the plane. In fact, it implied that the plane was expected.

Ginger lay still, resolved now to learn as much as he could before returning to the others. He had not long to wait. The plane passed low overhead and made a smooth landing on the lake, finishing its run not far from the camp. Men ran from the fire and dragged the machine still nearer. Two men got out and walked into the camp, where another man, evidently the leader of the ground party, was standing a little apart from the others.

The first words spoken by the newcomers struck Ginger like an electric shock, for they were in German, in which language the leader of the ground party replied. Stiff with amazement and dismay, Ginger heard one of the newcomers speak again, and at the sound of the voice the muscles in his throat seemed to restrict. The voice was unmistakable. It could belong to only one man. He had heard it too often to have any doubt about it. It was the one man whom they had most cause to fear – their old enemy, Hauptmann Erich von Stalhein, head of the Special Branch of the German Secret Service.

What on earth could have brought von Stalhein to a place like this was the thought that flashed into Ginger's head. The answer to the question was almost automatic. Obviously he had come to recover the missing portfolio.

For a few minutes longer Ginger watched; then the leaders went into the tent, and as soon as he realised that he was unlikely to gather any further information, he slid back off the rise and raced to the machine.

The others were still asleep, but he awakened them with scant ceremony.

'Biggles!' he cried tersely, shaking Biggles's shoulder. 'Hi! Wake up. Things are happening – get a move on.'

The others scrambled hastily to their feet, for there was a vibrant ring in Ginger's voice that bespoke real urgency.

'What is it?' asked Biggles sharply.

'There's a party of Russians on the other side of the hill. What's more, von Stalhein is with them.'

'What?'

'It's a fact.' Ginger described swiftly and briefly what he had seen.

For a moment even Biggles was speechless in the face of this astounding – not to say alarming – piece of information. 'My sainted aunt!' he muttered, 'this is developing into a more desperate business than I bargained for. How far away are they?'

'Only about a mile. If they happen to march this way they'd be right on us before we could do a thing.'

'All right – all right. Don't get excited. We shall have to do something about this. Let me think.'

For a few minutes there was silence while Biggles stared intently at the floor, deep in thought. At last he looked up. 'Von Stalhein is on the same job as we are, that's certain,' he said. 'If we take off he'll hear us. Further, he'd hear us every time we tried to get down anywhere near here. In short, once we're in the air we're stumped.'

'If we stay here and they happen to find us, we shall be knocked for six,' put in Algy grimly.

'You needn't tell me that,' returned Biggles crisply. 'As I see it, our only chance is to get this party on the run before they know we're about. If we could do that it ought to give us a little while to carry on the search unmolested.'

'Yes, but how are you going to do that?'

'There's only one way. We've got to attack them.'

'Attack them!' cried Algy. 'Four against forty? You're crazy.'

'Not so crazy as you might think. We've got two machine-guns and a couple of rifles. The enemy won't know that there are only four of us. Suppose you were in that camp, unaware of a hostile force in the district; then, suddenly, from close range, a brisk fire was opened up on you by machine-guns and rifles. What would you do?'

'Run,' answered Algy promptly.

'Exactly. Those Ruskys will run, too. They'll suppose that they're being attacked by one of those flying columns of Finns that have been doing so much damage lately. In their anxiety to get away they'll abandon their stores. We'll destroy them, which means that since they can't stay here without food or shelter they'll have to return to where they can get fresh supplies. While they're doing that we shall take the opportunity of finding the papers.'

'It sounds easy,' agreed Algy dubiously.

'Isn't it a bit thick to open fire on a sleeping camp?' put in Ginger.

Biggles laughed sarcastically. 'What d'you think this is – a Sunday-school party? Forget it. This is war, and a surprise attack is what every general dreams about. D'you suppose that if they'd tumbled on us they'd have invited us to pick up our guns and fire the first volley? Not on your life. After the trouble we've caused him in the past, if von Stalhein got hold of us he'd shoot us with no more qualms than if we were rabbits – you know that as well as I do. This is a chance we may not get again, and I'm in favour of taking advantage of it. One thing is certain – we've got to drive them out before they drive us out; otherwise we might as well pack up and go home.'

'I think we ought to give them a chance,' protested Ginger. 'After all, as long as we can get rid of them, that's really all we're concerned with.'

Biggles thought for a moment. 'Maybe you're right,' he said slowly. 'If we wounded any of them, we should find ourselves cluttered up with prisoners – unless we just left them to die, which isn't a nice thought. I'll tell you what. We'll try shooting high first. If they bolt, so well and good, but if they return our fire we shall have to let 'em have it, and no argument. After all, it's our lives against theirs.'

'What about von Stalhein's plane?' inquired Algy.

'We'll attend to that at the same time,' declared Biggles. 'A can of petrol should do the trick. Come on, let's get the guns out.'

In ten minutes they were ready, armed with the two mobile machine-guns they had brought with them, rifles and revolvers, in addition to which Biggles carried a two-gallon can of petrol with the cap already loosened.

From the spot where Ginger had lain they surveyed the enemy camp and saw that it was now sleeping; at least, only one man could be seen, a sentry, who, with a fine indifference to his task, was standing near the fire warming his hands. A yellow light showed through the canvas of the tent von Stalhein had entered.

Biggles gave his orders in a whisper. 'You stay here,' he told the others. 'I'm going to make a detour to get to the plane from the far side. As soon as you see the flames, let drive at the tops of the tents – and keep on firing. Yell at the same time. Try to make as much noise as a squadron of cavalry. I shall probably be about a quarter of an hour.' He glided away below the brow of the hill and was soon lost to sight.

Algy took one machine-gun and Smyth the other. They aligned them on the tents. Ginger had to be content with a rifle. After that there was nothing they could do except wait. The minutes passed slowly. Not a sound broke the silence.

'The fireworks are about due to begin I think,' murmured Algy at last.

Hardly had the words left his lips when a blue flicker of flame lit up the air over the machine. It grew swiftly in volume; then came a *whoosh*, and a great sheet of flame leapt skyward.

'Okay,' snapped Algy, 'let 'em rip.'

Instantly the still air was shattered with the demoniac rattle of machine-guns. After the silence the din was terrifying. Above the clatter rose the yells of the attackers. The blaze of the now burning aircraft, and the crackle of the bullets in its guns, added to the turmoil.

The effect on the camp was only what was to be expected in the circumstances. Utter confusion reigned. Blind panic followed, and in less than a minute the Russians were in flight, streaming across the snow with bullets whistling about their ears. Never was victory more swiftly or more easily achieved. Complete success had crowned the enterprise.

Biggles dashed up. 'Cease fire,' he ordered. 'They've gone and we'd better go steady with the ammunition.'

They waited for a little while to give the Russians a chance to get clear, and then went down to the camp.

'See what's on those sledges,' ordered Biggles. 'If there's nothing of any use to us pitch them on the fire. Do the same with the tents.' He himself went to the tent in which von Stalhein had been in consultation with the Russian leader. He came out stuffing some papers in his pocket, and then helped the others to drag the tent to the fire. In a few minutes all that remained of the enemy camp was a blazing pyre in the centre of an area of trampled snow. Most of the enemy had abandoned their rifles in their haste, and these, too, were flung into the blaze. The plane was a glowing heap of metal.

'I fancy that's cramped their style for a bit, anyway,' remarked Biggles with satisfaction as he surveyed the scene. 'We may as well get back to the machine.'

'What are you going to do next?' asked Algy as they approached the Blenheim.

'As it must be pretty nearly morning, we may as well go on with the search,' returned Biggles. 'I'll just have a look at these papers first.'

Reaching the machine, the others gathered round while Biggles examined the documents he had found in the enemy camp. All except one were in Russian, so as he could not read them he buried them in the snow. The exception was in German, and this he perused with interest, for there was good reason to suppose that it had been brought by von Stalhein.

Actually, it told them little they did not already know. It described the dead professor, referred to the papers containing the results of his experiments, and gave vague directions for finding them. It included a sketch-map showing the position where the professor's body had been found, proving that – as Biggles had surmised – the body had been located the day before by the Messerschmitt pilot. But there was, of course, no guide to the actual locality of the missing papers, for this was something the professor did not know himself, and Biggles derived a crumb of comfort from the fact that the enemy was in as big a quandary as he was regarding their whereabouts.

Having read the letter aloud, Biggles folded it and put it in his pocket. 'That doesn't help us much,' he remarked. 'The only thing we can do is to proceed as we did yesterday; but we'd better keep our eyes skinned for any stray Russians who may be about. Von Stalhein of course will come back. He's that sort of fellow.'

'By gosh! Won't he be in a tearing rage, too,' remarked Ginger.

'As he's three parts a rattlesnake at any time, I don't see that he can be much worse,' returned Biggles. 'We'd better keep clear of him if we can.'

'How far will those Russians have to go for fresh stores, d'you think?' queried Ginger.

'I don't know,' answered Biggles. 'I don't think it can be less than a couple of days' march. Come on, let's get busy while we've got the chance.'

CHAPTER III

Success – and Disaster

For the whole of that day they pursued their quest with energy and speed, knowing that it was only a question of time before von Stalhein would return with reinforcements – to say nothing of sending aircraft to locate them. And it was for this very reason that Biggles concentrated his efforts in an easterly direction – that is to say, over Russia, feeling that it was the most difficult as well as the most likely locality. They could, he reasoned, fall back inside the Finnish frontier and carry on the search there when they were seriously interfered with by von Stalhein.

It was about four o'clock, and they were circling in the Blenheim looking for a suitable place to pass the night, when Biggles's ever watchful eyes noticed an unusual scar that ran in a straight line across the untrodden snow, and coming lower, he soon saw that it was a track made by a body of men. The line it took gave him a clue to the identity of those who had made it, for the line came from the scene of the camp which they had attacked. Coming still lower – so low, indeed, that his wheels were only a few feet from the ground – he perceived that the track had been made by the Russians subsequent to the attack, and not on their outward journey, a fact that he deduced from the absence of sledge-marks. He pointed this out to Algy.

'We do at least know which way they've gone,' he remarked.

'How about following the track to see how far they've got?' suggested Algy.

'Good idea. It may give us a line on where they are making for, and consequently let us know roughly how long we may expect to be free from interference.'

Biggles was climbing steeply, following the track, when suddenly he gave a cry. He said nothing, but Algy was not long spotting what had called forth the exclamation. Some distance ahead the track started to traverse a long, narrow lake. But it did not proceed very far. It turned at right angles and made straight for the bank, where the snow was all trampled down as if a halt had been made.

An unpleasant sensation crept over Biggles as he circled low over the spot. Already in his heart he knew the reason for the sudden turn in the line of march, and why the halt had been made, but he hoped that he was wrong.

'What can you see down there?' he asked Algy in a curious voice.

Algy threw him a sidelong glance. 'It's no use kidding ourselves,' he said evenly. 'That's a crashed aeroplane under that pile of snow; you can see that from the shape of it.'

'Then it looks as if von Stalhein has tumbled on what we were looking for – by accident.'

'It looks that way, but there's still a chance that it isn't the Polish machine – or if it is, that von Stalhein didn't find the papers,' said Algy, trying to be optimistic.

Biggles said no more. He cut the throttle, landed on the ice, and taxied up the track made by the Russians to the wreck. Without a moment's hesitation, such was his

27

anxiety, he jumped down, and closely followed by Algy, ran to the scene of the trampled snow. In the centre of it, still half buried, although a good deal of the snow had been dragged away, was the remains of a crashed aeroplane. Biggles tore more of the snow from one of the crumpled wings and exposed Polish military markings.

'That settles any argument about that,' he asserted harshly, and remembering the professor's instructions for finding the papers, he ran straight to the spot. His heart was sick with anxiety, for footmarks were everywhere, and it was obvious that the search had been thorough. He knew only too well that von Stalhein was nothing if not efficient. Within a minute he knew the grim truth, for exactly where the professor had described it was a large rock. Around it the snow had been trampled. Under the rock was a cavity, but it was empty. The portfolio had gone. Presently they found it, half buried in the snow a little distance away. The flap was open. It was empty.

Biggles took out a cigarette and tapped it on the back of his hand. 'What d'you know about that?' he said bitterly. 'Von Stalhein never had a bigger stroke of luck in his life. He must have been going across the lake when he spotted the crash. The irritating part of it is, if we had left him to go on searching where he was when we attacked him, the chances are that he wouldn't have found it. That was ten miles from here. The poor old professor no doubt meant well, but actually he couldn't have chosen a worse hiding-place. It was so obvious. The rock was so conspicuous.'

Algy, too, lit a cigarette. 'All the same, I don't see where else he could have hidden it,' he said slowly. 'He couldn't very well just tuck it into the snow, where it would have been exposed as soon as the stuff melted. Well, it certainly is von Stalhein's lucky day. As far as we're concerned – well, it's a tough break. Von Stalhein wins the game after all.'

'What d'you mean – wins the game?' snapped Biggles. 'This is only the first round. He can't have got back to his base yet, and while he's walking about Russia with those papers on him he can't claim to have won – not while we're still on our feet, anyway.'

Ginger and Smyth had come up. They did not need telling what had happened. The picture told its own story.

'It looks as if this is where we go home,' observed Ginger.

'On the contrary, this is where we go after von Stalhein,' returned Biggles curtly.

Algy smiled wanly. 'Biggles old top, there are moments when I wonder seriously if you didn't crack your skull in one of your crashes.'

'Meaning what?'

'You're daft to think of tackling—'

'You said that last night,' cut in Biggles.

'I know, but it's one thing to attack a sleeping camp, and quite another for us to take on that bunch of stiffs in cold blood. There can't be less than forty of them.'

'You haven't forgotten that when they bolted quite a number of them left their rifles behind?'

'No, I haven't forgotten that either.'

Biggles's face was grim. 'I'm going to get those papers, or—'

'Or what?'

'Oh, stop arguing. Let's get going.'

They hastened back to the Blenheim and got aboard. Just what Biggles was going to do he didn't say. Possibly he wasn't sure himself.

His first action was to locate the Russians, and, since they were on foot, this did not take long. The party appeared as a small black column moving slowly across the waste of snow. As soon as he saw it Biggles turned away.

'They'll have heard us,' remarked Algy.

'Possibly, but we're too far off for them to recognise the machine,' answered Biggles. 'Bear in mind that ours isn't the only plane hereabouts. For all they know it may be one of their own.' As he spoke Biggles turned away from the track at right angles.

He flew on for about five minutes, during which time the Blenheim had covered ten miles. Then he turned sharp left, flew for another five or six minutes, and then left again, a manoeuvre which, if the Russians had held on their course, put him well in front of them. From a thousand feet he started to examine the ground carefully, and apparently he found what he was looking for, for he turned away and landed on a convenient lake, running the machine on until it was close against the sagging pines that came down on all sides to the edge of the ice.

'Get the guns out,' he ordered crisply, and the weapons that had been used for the attack on the camp were again produced.

'Start cutting some sticks – straight ones if possible,' was Biggles's next command.

'What's the idea?' inquired Algy, taking out his pocket-knife.

'You'll see,' returned Biggles briefly.

It took them about a quarter of an hour to find a dozen good sticks and strip them of their twigs. Biggles then gathered them under his arm, picked up a rifle, and telling the others to follow with the rest of the weapons, set off on a course that, as Algy soon realised, would intercept that of the Russians. A halt was called while Biggles climbed to the top of a hill to reconnoitre. He soon came running back.

'It's all right,' he said, 'they're coming. This way.'

A short walk brought them to a narrow depression between two banks, rather after the manner of a railway cutting. To enhance this effect, through it ran a number of lines in the snow, obviously the tracks of sledges.

'This must be the track the Russians made on their outward journey,' Biggles explained. 'I spotted it from the air, and unless my judgement is at fault, the Russians are now cutting across to strike it, obviously with the intention of returning along it. The party should therefore pass through this cutting – in fact, they're already within a mile of us. I'm going to ambush them here. Algy, you'll take one of the machine-guns and stay where you are. Ginger, you take a rifle and get behind those rocks on the other side. Smyth, you take the other machine-gun and find a place near Ginger. Don't let yourselves be seen. For the love of Mike keep your heads down until I give the signal.'

Biggles waited for the others to take up their allotted positions, and then, picking up the sticks, he worked them horizontally into the snow along each side of the cutting, pointing slightly downwards until they gave a fair representation of rifles covering the track. He then went down to judge the effect, and came back announcing that it was even better than he had hoped. He then took up his own position, one from which he could watch the approach of the Russians without being seen. 'No shooting unless I give the word,' he told the others. 'Show yourselves when I go down to have a word with von Stalhein.'

'Watch out he doesn't plug you,' warned Ginger anxiously.

'He'd be a fool to do that, with nearly twenty rifles covering him,' grinned Biggles. 'If I know von Stalhein, he's got more sense than to commit suicide.'

They hadn't long to wait. Ten minutes later the Russians came into view, marching in column of fours, about forty men in all. Von Stalhein, with the Russian leader, a man conspicuous by his height, and another officer in German uniform, presumably the pilot of von Stalhein's plane, stalked along just ahead of the main body.

Biggles smiled faintly as they strode unsuspecting into the trap, for it was a situation after his own heart. He waited until they were within a score of paces, and then stood up.

'Halt!' he called crisply in German. 'Von Stalhein, tell those men to drop their weapons. One shot, and I'll tell my men to mow you down where you stand. You're covered by machine-guns.'

Von Stalhein's hand flashed to his pocket, but he did not draw the weapon he obviously had in it. His blue eyes moved slowly round the half circle of supposed weapons that menaced him.

Algy got on his knees and dragged his machine-gun into view. Smyth did the same. Ginger, too, could be seen. There was no reason why von Stalhein should for one moment doubt the truth of Biggles's assertion. The Russians stood still, like a flock of sheep, staring at the ridge.

Biggles walked down the slope into the gully. Von Stalhein watched him, his eyes on Biggles's face. His own face was expressionless.

'We've met in some queer places, but I little thought that we should bump into each other in this out-of-the-world spot,' began Biggles pleasantly, as he strolled up to the German. 'But there,' he added, 'I suppose it's only natural that we should so often find ourselves on the same job. I shouldn't have troubled you, though, if you hadn't been lucky enough to strike by accident what we were both looking for.'

'Major Bigglesworth,' said von Stalhein coldly, 'there are times when I seriously wonder if you were created by the devil just to annoy me. I confess that nobody was farther from my thoughts at this moment.'

'And nobody was farther from my thoughts than you, until you dropped into the game a few hours ago,' replied Biggles. 'It was like old times to hear your voice again.'

'Then it was you who attacked our camp last night?'

'Yes, but I don't think attacked is the right word.'

'What do you mean?'

'Well, we took care not to hurt you. You don't suppose that it was by accident that all our shots went over your heads, do you? I know that isn't your way of doing things, but as I told you once before, I should be genuinely sorry if anything happened to you – you're always the life and soul of the party. But we're wasting time. You must be anxious to get back, and so am I. D'you mind handing over the papers?'

'What papers?'

Biggles looked pained. 'Really, von Stalhein, it isn't like you to start that childish sort of talk. Don't make me resort to violence – you know how I hate it. It's my turn to call the tune. Pass them over and look pleasant.'

Von Stalhein's eyes never left Biggles's face. He allowed a frosty smile to part his lips. 'Yes,' he agreed bitingly, 'it's your turn to call the tune, but the game isn't over yet.' He put his hand in his breast pocket and produced a bulky envelope with the flap loose.

Biggles took the papers and glanced through them to make sure that they were what he was looking for. Satisfied that they were, he put them in his own pocket. 'Thanks,' he said, 'I won't detain you any longer. Go right ahead.' Biggles looked up at the ridge. 'All right,' he called, 'let them pass, but at the first sign of treachery open fire.' He stood aside.

Von Stalhein bowed, smiling sardonically. 'We shall meet again before very long I think,' he predicted.

'The pleasure will be yours,' smiled Biggles. '*Auf Wiedersehen.*'

Von Stalhein said something Biggles did not understand, presumably in Russian, to the leader of the party, who, while this conversation had been going on, had not said a word. His face expressed a mixture of consternation and amazement. However, he gave an order and the party moved forward. Von Stalhein did not glance back. They went on through the gully, and soon the party was again a black column tramping across the snow.

Biggles beckoned to the others and they hastened to join him.

'Nice work, laddie,' grinned Algy.

'Not so bad,' smiled Biggles. 'Let's get back to the machine. The sooner we're out of this the better I shall be pleased. There's a look in von Stalhein's eye that I don't like.'

'But what could he do now?'

'I don't know, but I've a feeling that he's got something up his sleeve.'

34

'D'you suppose that he's sent somebody on ahead for reinforcements – I mean, before we stopped him?'

'Don't ask me, but it struck me that he wasn't so upset as he ought to have been. Let's go. Once we get in the machine he can do what he likes. Ten minutes should see us on our way.'

That a lot can happen in ten minutes Biggles was well aware, but he was certainly not prepared for what was to happen in the next short interval of time. In fact, the success of the mission seemed assured.

Twilight was closing in as they started back, a cold, eerie half-light that spread like a stain from the west over the dreary scene. Even the trees, drooping under their weight of snow, seemed to bow under the dismal depression that hung over everything like a blanket.

The airmen reached the Blenheim without misadventure, and Biggles was just opening the door when from the east came the low, ominous rumble of heavy bombers. At first the sound was no more than a deep vibrant purr that rose and fell in the still air, but it increased rapidly in volume, and it was obvious that the bombers were heading directly towards the spot where the airmen stood staring up into the sky.

'There they are,' said Biggles, pointing.

'Five of 'em,' muttered Algy, following the direction of Biggles's outstretched finger. 'We'd better push off.'

'You're right,' agreed Biggles tersely. 'Von Stalhein must have sent a messenger on ahead, or somehow got in touch with an aerodrome. From the way they're flying, these big boys are looking for us. Let's go!'

Later on Biggles felt that he made a mistake in taking off as he did, for had the machine remained stationary there was a good chance that it would not have been seen.

But it is easy to be wise after an event. The truth of the matter was – and Biggles in his heart knew it – that with the menace drawing swiftly nearer, he took off in too great a hurry. He did not fail to survey the line of his take-off before opening the throttle, for this was automatic, but instead of his usual intense scrutiny, he gave the surface of the lake no more than a cursory glance. It may have been that as, during the last twenty-four hours, he had made a dozen landings and take-offs from frozen lakes without seeing anything in the nature of an obstacle, he subconsciously took it for granted that this one would be no different from the rest. Be that as it may, Algy was no sooner in his seat than he opened the throttle, for by this time the bombers were nearly overhead.

It was not until the Blenheim was racing tail up across the ice at fifty miles an hour that he saw the little pile of snow directly in his path. For an instant he stared at it, trying to make out what it was, hoping that it was only soft snow; then, in a flash, he knew the truth, and it was the shape of the snow that revealed it. A floating branch or log had been frozen in the ice, and against it the snow had drifted.

Now to change the course of an aircraft travelling at high speed over the ground is a highly dangerous thing to do at any time; the strain on the undercarriage becomes enormous, and is transmitted to the whole machine. The designer cannot make allowances for such strains, and stresses the machine on the assumption that it will take off in a straight line.

As far as Biggles was concerned, it was one of those occasions when a pilot has no time to think. His reaction is instinctive, and whether or not he gets away with it depends a good deal on luck as well as skill. Thus was it with Biggles. To stop was impossible. To try to lift the machine over the obstacle before he had got up flying speed would be to invite disaster. Yet, at the same time, to touch either of his brakes would be equally fatal; so he pressed the rudder-bar lightly with his left foot, hoping that it would give him just enough turning movement to clear the obstacle. Had the machine been on a normal aerodrome he might have succeeded, but on ice it was a different matter. Instantly the Blenheim started to skid, and once started there was no stopping it. It did what would have been impossible on turf. Propelled by the sheer weight it carried, the machine kept on its course, but in a sideways position.

Knowing that a crash was inevitable, and with the fear of fire ever in the background of his mind, Biggles flicked off the ignition switch, and a split second later one of the wheels struck the log. The result was what might have been foreseen. The undercarriage was torn clean away, while the machine, buckled under the force of the collision, was hurled aside. There was a splintering, tearing series of crashes as the metal propellers bit into the ice and hurled it into the air like the jet from a fountain. The fuselage, flat on the ice, with one wing trailing, spun sickeningly for a hundred yards before coming to a stop.

No one moves faster than a pilot after a crash – that is, of course, assuming he is able to move. He is only too well aware that a fractured petrol-lead and one spark kicked out of a dying magneto can result in a sheet of flame from which nothing can save him.

Biggles flung Algy off his lap, where he had been hurled by the collision, and yelling to the others, fell out onto the ice. Algy followed. Ginger, wiping blood from his nose with his sleeve, tumbled out of the centre turret. Biggles dashed to the tail seat. Smyth was in a heap on the floor. They dragged him out, moaning and gasping for breath.

'He's only winded, I think,' said Biggles tersely, kneeling by the mechanic and running his hands over him.

Smyth, still gasping, tried to sit up. 'I'm all right,' he panted.

In the panic of the moment they had all forgotten the bombers, even though their roaring now seemed to shake the earth.

Ginger was the first to turn his face upwards. 'Look!' he screamed.

From each of the bombers men were falling, one after the other, turning over and over in the air. Then their parachutes started to open, and a swarm of fabric mushrooms floated earthward. The sky seemed to be full of them. Biggles calculated that there were at least fifty.

For a moment nobody spoke. There seemed to be nothing to say. The awful truth was all too plain to see, for already the parachutists were dropping onto the ice and, freeing themselves of their harness, were converging on the crash.

CHAPTER IV

A Grim Ultimatum

Biggles's first thought was of the papers in his pocket. He remembered Colonel Raymond's words: 'At all costs they must not be allowed to fall into the hands of the enemy.' Yet even then he hesitated to destroy them, for once burnt they were gone for ever, and with the professor dead, the vital information they contained could never be recovered. He realised, too, that the papers would directly affect their own fate. Once they fell into von Stalhein's hands his first precaution would be to silence those who might, if they escaped, say what had become of them. On the other hand, without the papers von Stalhein would hesitate to destroy the only people who knew where they were.

Yet where could they be hidden? All round the ice lay flat and bare, and to attempt to hide them in the wreck of the machine would be as futile as if he had retained them on his person. There seemed to be only one way, and Biggles seized upon it. In the crash one of the wings had collapsed, with the result that an engine had broken loose from its bearers; the manifold exhaust had snapped off, and had slid some thirty or forty yards from the machine, where, being hot, it had already half buried itself in the thick ice which, of course, had partly melted. It was obvious that in a few seconds the manifold would disappear from sight altogether; but as it grew cold the water would quickly freeze again and entomb it.

In a moment Biggles tore a piece of loose fabric from the damaged wing, wrapped the papers in it, and hastening to the pool of water that marked the spot where the manifold was swiftly disappearing, he threw the manifold aside and into the water-filled cavity it had created he dropped the packet, forcing it to sink under the weight of his automatic, which would in any case, he knew, soon be taken from him. This done, he marked the spot by taking a line on landmarks on either bank, and then rejoined the others, who were still standing by the crash waiting for him to give them a lead.

Resistance was clearly out of the question. It would have been suicidal, for they were completely encircled by the Russians who had dropped from the sky and were now closing in on them. It is true that they could have put up a fight, for they were well armed, but the end of such a one-sided affair would have been a foregone conclusion. Even if the Russians were driven off they would only have to line the banks of the lake to starve them into submission.

Biggles was anxious to avoid being killed, if it were possible, for more reasons than one; and one reason was the papers. He alone knew where they were hidden, and if he failed to return, that would be the end of any chance of their ultimately reaching home. While he was still alive, whatever the Russians might do, there was still a hope – a slender one admittedly, but even that was better than no hope at all – that he might one day return and recover the papers. A bullet whizzing over the ice decided him, and he put his hands up.

'It's no use,' he told the others. 'We can't fight this mob. We shall have to surrender.'

Algy looked surprised, for the decision was not like Biggles; however, he did not question the order, but slowly raised his hands. The others did the same, including Smyth, who was now nearly normal. The Russians closed in, and Biggles, looking round the circle, saw that von Stalhein was not with them.

'What have you done with the papers?' asked Algy.

'I've hidden them,' returned Biggles.

'Where?'

'Never mind. If you don't know, the information can't be got out of you,' replied Biggles evenly. 'I may tell you later on.'

The Russians now came up and crowded round the prisoners, who were quickly disarmed. Their pockets, too, were emptied, everything being put into the leader's haversack. Whether this man was an officer or an N.C.O. Biggles could not make out, for as they had no common language conversation was not possible. However, he didn't seem badly disposed towards them; in fact, after looking at the crash, he shrugged his shoulders and smiled sympathetically at the British airmen. Several of the Russians gathered round the log that had caused the disaster, for they, as parachutists, knew a good deal about flying, and understood exactly what had happened.

While this had been going on the five bombers had circled, slowly descending, and now they landed one after the other on the ice, afterwards taxiing into position for a take-off near the crashed Blenheim. There was a fairly long delay while the Blenheim was searched from end to end, the maps going into the Russian leader's haversack. There then appeared to be a discussion between him and the pilots of the bombers as to the disposal of the stores, armament, and equipment. From their gestures Biggles was able to follow the debate fairly well, and he formed the opinion that the pilots were unwilling to carry so much extra weight – a supposition that was confirmed when they all moved off, leaving the crash exactly as it lay.

Night had now fallen, and while it was not really dark, Biggles hoped that camp would be made and the take-off postponed until the next morning, for this would give them a chance to escape – not a very good chance perhaps, but a better chance than they would have once they had been handed over to von Stalhein, who would, he felt sure, claim them when he heard of their capture.

In this hope, however, Biggles was to be disappointed, for the whole party moved over to the big machines, where the British airmen were separated, presumably to distribute the weight. The bombers then took off and roared away in an easterly direction.

The flight, as near as Biggles could judge, lasted only about twenty minutes, in which time he estimated that they had covered about fifty miles. They then glided down and landed. Looking through a window, Biggles could see landing lights put out to guide them, from which he supposed that they were not at a regular aerodrome. This, he presently saw, was only half correct. The place was evidently used as an aircraft base, but canvas hangars suggested that it was only a temporary and not a permanent aerodrome. For the rest, in the short time he had to survey the scene after he had got out of the plane he saw that the landing-ground was, in fact, yet another lake, but one so large that the extremities were lost in the distance. He thought it might be Lake Onega, which, next to Lake Ladoga, was the largest lake in the district.

At the point where they had landed the bank rose steeply for a hundred feet or more, and it was at the base of a rocky hill that the hangars had been erected. A short distance to the right the lights of a village, or a small town, glowed dimly, and above, silhouetted against the sky, he could see an imposing fort or citadel. He could not make out the details, but at any rate it was a massive building of considerable size, and this, he suspected – correctly, as he soon discovered – was their destination.

He was relieved when he was joined by the others, for he was afraid they might be separated, and under an armed guard the party moved forward between the hangars to a road that wound a serpentine course upwards towards the fort. A march of some twenty minutes brought them to it, when it became possible to see that it was a medieval-looking structure rising sheer out of rock which had obviously been used in its construction. At a gloomy portal they were challenged by a sentry, but after a brief halt they moved forward again. Heavy gates clanged behind them.

'I know now what it must feel like to be taken into Dartmoor,' murmured Algy.

'Judging from the outside of this place, Dartmoor is a luxury hotel compared with it,' growled Ginger. 'If we can crack our way out of this joint we need never fear being locked up anywhere.'

The Russian leader made it clear by gestures that they must not talk, a command that was obeyed, for the man had not treated them badly.

Their way now lay through a series of stone corridors, cold and depressing, lighted by an occasional lantern.

Another sentry met them and conducted them on, their echoing footsteps adding to the atmosphere of gloom. The sentry halted before a heavy, iron-studded door; he knocked on it and, in answer to a command from within, opened it. A shaft of bright yellow light fell athwart the corridor. The leader of the party that had captured them beckoned to the prisoners and entered the room, carrying in his hand the haversack containing their personal belongings. This he placed on a great, antique table; he then saluted and withdrew, closing the door behind him.

There were three men in the room – two, judging from their uniforms, being Russian officers. The third was von Stalhein. He eyed Biggles with a whimsical smile, in which, however, there was more triumph than humour.

'I told you the game was only beginning,' he said with a sneer, in his perfect English.

Biggles nodded. 'Go ahead,' he invited. 'It's your lead – but don't get the idea that this is the end of the game.'

'Nearly – very nearly,' said the German softly. 'This is the last hand. It was unfortunate for you that I had the foresight to send a man on ahead of my party to fetch the bombers.'

Von Stalhein pulled the haversack towards him and emptied the contents on the table. He went through them quickly, but without finding what he sought. Again he raised his cold blue eyes to Biggles's face. 'Where are the papers?' he demanded curtly.

'What papers?' returned Biggles blandly, using the same words that von Stalhein had used earlier in the day.

The German smiled grimly. 'I get your meaning,' he said. 'But don't forget I was polite enough to hand the papers over.'

'So would I – if I had them,' answered Biggles evenly.

The Russian who had captured them was brought back into the room and closely questioned for some time. As soon as he had gone von Stalhein turned again to Biggles.

'Where did you put them?' he demanded in a manner that was now frankly hostile. 'They weren't on your person and they weren't in the machine. What did you do with them?'

'That's a fair question so I'll give you a fair answer,' countered Biggles. 'I hid them. They now repose in a place where – unless I am flattering myself – you will never find them.'

The German's eyes switched to Algy, and then to Ginger.

'It's no use looking at them,' remarked Biggles quietly. 'They don't know where they are. Such a vital piece of information I kept to myself.'

Von Stalhein toyed with his monocle for a moment. He fitted a cigarette into a long holder, lit it, and sent a cloud of grey smoke curling towards the ceiling. 'You know, Bigglesworth, in the past you've had a lot of luck,' he said reflectively.

'Now don't try to do me out of what little credit my efforts have brought me,' protested Biggles.

'But luck,' continued von Stalhein imperturbably, 'can't last for ever, and I think you've about come to the end of it. You've given me more trouble than the rest of the British Intelligence Service put together, and I find you irritating. Still, there are qualities about you that I, who try to be efficient, admire, and for that reason I'm going to give you a chance. Tell me where the papers are and I will see that you are handed over to the authorities as ordinary prisoners of war. Refuse, and I'll see to it that you're shot for carrying arms against a nation with whom you are not at war.'

'We seem to have had this argument before,' replied Biggles. 'We are British subjects – yes; as such we are volunteers in Finland, a fact that is borne out by the Finnish uniforms we are wearing. Among those papers on the table you will find our commissions in the Finnish Air Force; by International Law they make us belligerents, and in the event of capture we claim the privileges of prisoners of war.'

Von Stalhein picked up the documents in question. He rolled them into a ball and deliberately dropped it into the fire. 'They are easily disposed of,' he said quietly. 'Let us now assume that you are not fighting for Finland, but are acting as spies for the British Government.'

'Have it your own way,' murmured Biggles. 'But I still hold the trump card. Shoot us, and you've lost the papers for ever.'

Von Stalhein stroked his chin. 'I wonder,' he said softly. 'It rather looks as if I shall have to employ more persuasive methods. I am going to give you until eight o'clock tomorrow morning to remember where you put those papers; if by that time you have not recovered your memory, then your companions will be taken into the courtyard and shot. Since they don't know where the papers are there is really no point in my keeping them here. I will see that you get a room overlooking the court-yard, so that you will be able to watch the proceedings. I think you know me well enough to appreciate that when I say a thing I mean it. In effect, you will sign your friends' death warrants. Think it over. That's all – until eight o'clock.'

'You might see that we get a respectable dinner,' requested Biggles. 'We've had a busy day and we're hungry.'

'I'll attend to it,' promised von Stalhein. 'By the way, where are the rest of your men?'

'What men?'

'The crowd you had with you when you took the papers from me.'

'Oh, those! There weren't any men – just the four of us. The rest of the rifles were sticks.'

Von Stalhein started. A pink flush stained his pale cheeks and his lips pressed themselves together in a straight line. It was clear that, being entirely German and lacking in sense of humour, he hated the manner in which he had been tricked. 'Very clever,' he sneered. 'But not clever enough. We'll see who laughs last.'

'Yes, we shall see,' agreed Biggles.

The Russian guard was called and the prisoners were led away.

After traversing several corridors, slowly mounting, they were shown into a large, sparsely furnished apartment with a number of trestle beds arranged round the walls, with blankets folded at their heads. It seemed that the place had been used before as a prison cell, but there were no other prisoners. A deal table stood in the middle of the room, and on it an iron bowl and a can of water. There was only one window; it was heavily barred, and it overlooked a paved courtyard enclosed within high walls. In fact, the fort was built round the courtyard, but a flight of steps gave access to ramparts with which the whole was surrounded. So much the prisoners saw at a glance.

Biggles sat on one of the beds. 'It looks as if we're in a jam,' he announced.

'You're telling us!' muttered Algy.

'What's the matter? It isn't the first jam we've been in, is it?'

'No, but from what I can see you'll be a bright lad to get out of this one. It would have put the tin hat on Jack Sheppard's career as a prison-buster. What are we going to do?'

'Obviously, I'm going to show von Stalhein where the papers are hidden.'

'*What?*' There was a chorus of dissent.

'But don't be silly,' argued Biggles. 'You heard what von Stalhein said about bumping you off at eight o'clock? He'll do it too, as sure as fate, unless I tell him what he wants to know.'

'Well, let him,' declared Algy desperately.

'And you think I'm going to stand here and watch you lined up against a wall? Not if I can prevent it,' declared Biggles. 'I'm going to tell that rattlesnake that I shall have to *show* him where the papers are hidden, for I can't describe the place to him. I shall have to go myself – get the idea? That will give me a little longer to do something – perhaps a chance to get away.'

'For sheer cold-blooded optimism you certainly take the cake,' remarked Algy.

'Well, try to think of something better,' invited Biggles. 'Meanwhile we may as well get some sleep while we can.'

Reluctantly the others agreed.

CHAPTER V

Biggles Takes a Trip

They were up and washed, sitting on their beds the following morning when the door opened and von Stalhein, followed by two Russian guards, entered. Von Stalhein, as usual, was immaculate, and his monocle gleamed coldly. He addressed Biggles.

'Well?' was all he said.

Biggles nodded. 'All right, I agree,' he answered. 'You've got me in a tight spot and I can't refuse – you know that.'

The German smiled frostily. 'Where are the papers?'

'I can't tell you,' answered Biggles. 'Just a minute,' he went on quickly, as von Stalhein's face darkened with anger. 'Let me explain. I know where the papers are because I hid them, but I couldn't possibly describe the place to you because there was no feature, no landmark, to mark the spot. In the circumstances I can only suggest that you take me to the place, and then I'll show you where the papers are.'

'How far away is this place?'

'About fifty miles – quite close to where we were picked up. The best thing would be for you to fly me back to the lake where we crashed yesterday. From there it's a short walk through the snow. We ought to be able to get the papers and return here in a few hours.'

For a moment von Stalhein regarded Biggles suspiciously. 'Very well,' he agreed slowly, 'I will order an aeroplane immediately. But if you try any tricks...' His eyes narrowed.

'I'm not a madman,' protested Biggles. 'By the way, have I your word that if I hand you the papers you will treat us as prisoners of war?'

'That is what I said,' announced von Stalhein curtly.

In half an hour Biggles was getting into the machine – one of the big Russian bombers. In spite of his protests that it was unnecessary – for the German had provided an escort of six Russian soldiers – he had been handcuffed. But von Stalhein was taking no chances, and he refused to take them off. A small hand-sled, lightly loaded with what Biggles supposed to be food, was lifted aboard, and the machine took off. Twenty minutes later, under a leaden sky, it landed on the lake where the Blenheim still lay, a twisted wreck.

Biggles's brain had not been idle during the journey. He had no intention of taking von Stalhein straight to the spot where the papers now lay frozen in the ice, which was, as we know, only a short distance from the crash; but what had upset his plan was the handcuffs. With steel bracelets on his wrists he was absolutely helpless, so the first problem that exercised his mind was how to get rid of them.

'Well, where are they?' demanded von Stalhein as they got out. The Russians followed them, leaving the pilot sitting in his seat.

Biggles had, from the air, made a swift survey of the landscape. To his right, from the edge of the lake, the ground rose in a steep, snow-covered slope perhaps a hundred feet high. Beyond the ridge the ground dropped away into a valley nearly a mile wide, with an even steeper range of hills beyond, a formidable barrier that rose for several hundred feet, the whole being covered with smooth, untrodden snow.

Von Stalhein was waiting.

Biggles nodded towards the nearest ridge. 'That's the way we shall have to go,' he said.

'Good,' answered von Stalhein, and the party moved off, Biggles and the German walking in front, followed by two Russians dragging the sled, and then the remaining four guards with rifles over their arms.

Handicapped as he was by the handcuffs, Biggles had a job to get up the first slope; actually he made it appear much more difficult for him than it really was, floundering in the deep snow and sometimes falling, so that he had to be helped to his feet by the Russians, who seemed to sympathise with his plight, for even they found the going by no means easy. The consequence was, by the time they got to the ridge Biggles was puffing and blowing, and generally affecting all the symptoms of exhaustion.

Von Stalhein, now that they were so near their objective, got more and more impatient at every delay, particularly when Biggles insisted on resting before going on. 'Can't you see that I'm nearly all in?' he said plaintively. However, after a short spell he got on his feet, and after descending the far slope, set off across the valley.

'Where are we going?' demanded von Stalhein.

Biggles nodded towards the towering hills ahead. 'Just over the other side,' he answered.

Von Stalhein said no more, but stalked on, curbing his impatience as well as he could – which was not very well.

They crossed the valley, in the bottom of which the snow had drifted in places to a depth of three or four feet, and while the crust was frozen hard enough in most places to support their weight, sometimes it broke through, when Biggles had to be extricated. As a matter of fact, his frequent stumbles were deliberate in the hope that repeated delays would cause von Stalhein to release his hands. He took care not to suggest this himself, however, for fear the suspicions of the German were aroused. But still von Stalhein refused to take the bait.

The valley traversed, the ascent of the big hill commenced, and here Biggles was seriously handicapped. However, he puffed along, apparently making a genuine attempt to keep up with the party, which, naturally, had to lag back for him. Nearing the top the snow became harder, so hard, indeed, that it was little better than a sheet of ice, and the climbers had to dig their heels into it to get a foothold. Progress became little more than a snail's pace, and von Stalhein began to lose his temper. Twice Biggles slipped, and glissaded wildly for thirty or forty yards; on such occasions he lay gasping until the Russians came back, helped him to his feet, and literally dragged him up the slope to where von Stalhein was waiting.

Biggles knew that something had got to be done pretty soon, for all this time they were getting farther and farther away from the papers, and he could not keep up the deception much longer without von Stalhein becoming suspicious. They were now nearly at the top of the hill, and as he had no idea of what was going to happen when he got there, he determined on one last attempt to get his hands free. He slipped, and after staggering for a moment like a drunken man, he fell heavily and began to slide backwards. This time he really could not stop, so he covered his face with his arms and allowed himself to slide, thankful that there were no obstacles against which he might collide. He went halfway down the hill before he was brought to a stop by a patch of soft snow, and there he lay, exhausted – but not so exhausted as he pretended to be. He made no attempt to get up, so the party halted while two of the Russians came back and tried to get him on his feet. But Biggles flopped like a sack of flour, and since it was only with the greatest difficulty that the Russians could get him along at all, they shouted something to von Stalhein. What they said he did not know, but his heart gave a lurch when one of the guards smiled and hurried up to von Stalhein. Presently he returned, bringing with him the key of the handcuffs, which were removed. On the face of it, there was no real point in keeping them on, for he was one unarmed man among seven, six of whom carried rifles and the other an automatic.

Still playing for time, Biggles dragged himself wearily up the steep slope, and after a considerable delay reached the others who, with the exception of the German, were squatting on the snow, having turned the sled sideways on so that it could not run down. The men had leaned their rifles against it.

Reaching von Stalhein, Biggles collapsed in a heap, gasping for breath; but his eyes were taking in every detail of the situation, for the moment for which he had been waiting had arrived. Slowly, as if it were a tremendous effort, he began to get up. Then, suddenly, he moved like lightning. He jerked to his feet, slammed his right first against the German's jaw, knocking him over backwards, and dived at the sled. It took him only a split second to drag the nose round so that it was pointing down the hill.

The rifles, except one which he grabbed, he kicked aside. Then, flinging himself on the sled in a flying leap, he tore away down the hill.

In an instant he was travelling at a speed that alarmed him; but apprehensive of the shots that he knew would follow, he eased his weight a little to one side so that the sled swerved slightly. He was only just in time, for bullets zipped into the snow unpleasantly close to his side; but a small mark travelling at nearly sixty miles an hour is not easy to hit, and he made it more difficult by altering his weight so that his course was anything but straight. He did not attempt to look behind; he was much too concerned with where he was going, for a spill at such speed might have serious consequences. He took a small mound like a ski jumper, and grunted as he came down flat on his stomach; but the sled still tore on at dizzy speed, which ultimately carried him three parts of the way across the valley. His great regret was that the others couldn't see him, for it was the most exciting ride he had ever had in his life, and he made a mental note that he would take up tobogganing when he got too old for flying.

At last, as it met the gentle slope on the far side of the valley, the sled began to lose speed. He remained on it while it made any progress at all, but as soon as it had stopped he picked up the rifle, and smiling with the thrill of the mad ride and at the satisfactory outcome of his trip, he looked back across the valley. Von Stalhein and the Russians, looking like black ants, were slipping and sliding down his track more than a mile away. He abandoned the sled that had done him such good service and hurried on.

His one fear now was that the Russian pilot who had remained in the plane would have heard the shots, and reach the ridge in front of him first, to see what the shooting was about. Actually they arrived at the ridge together, but the Russian was unarmed – or at least, no weapon was visible. Almost colliding with Biggles, he merely stared in astonishment, evidently wondering, not without reason, how the miracle had been accomplished.

Biggles tapped the rifle meaningly, and then pointed to the opposite hill.

The pilot took the tip; he was in no position to argue. In any case, he did not seem particularly concerned about the affair, feeling, perhaps, that it was not his business to worry about a prisoner. He nodded pleasantly and walked on to meet his comrades. Biggles watched him for a little while to make sure that there was no hanky-panky, but seeing that he did not even look back, he turned towards the lake and, reaching the ice, made for the spot where he had hidden the papers. There was no difficulty in finding it, for the ice was a slightly different colour where it had been melted.

Getting the papers out, however, was not such a simple matter, and in the end he achieved it by shattering the ice piecemeal with the butt of the rifle. He recovered his automatic at the same time, so having no further use for the rifle, he sent it spinning into the wreck of the Blenheim. Both the canvas-covered bundle of papers and the automatic had pieces of ice adhering to them, so he went over to the Russian bomber and laid them on one of the still warm engines to melt. He then went into the machine and examined the cockpit; he did this unhurriedly, knowing that von Stalhein and the Russians could not possibly get back to the ridge overlooking the lake in less than half an hour. What pleased him still more was the realisation that without an aircraft it would take von

Stalhein and the Russians at least two days to cover the fifty miles that lay between the lake and the fort.

Satisfied that the flying of the machine presented no difficulty, he fetched the papers and the pistol from the engine on which he had laid them, and was glad to see that they were now free from ice. He looked hard at the sky, which, from a dull leaden colour, had deepened to almost inky black. Subconsciously he had been aware of the fading light for some time, but now, with a flight before him, he regarded it with a different interest, and some apprehension. 'There's snow coming, if I know anything about weather,' he told himself. For a moment, but only for a moment, he was tempted to fly the papers straight back to Helsinki, but the idea of abandoning the others to the tender mercy of von Stalhein, who would, in view of what had happened, be more than usually vindictive, was so repugnant to him that he dismissed the thought instantly. He knew that none or all must be saved, or the rest of his life would be spent in remorse.

His plan, briefly, was to fly back to within a few miles of the fort, land the machine where there was little chance of its being found, and then, in some manner not yet decided, attempt to rescue the others, after which they would make for the plane and fly home together. Yet now even the elements seemed to be conspiring against him, for should snow begin to fall he was likely to lose himself. The machine was not equipped for blind flying, and in any case the country was absolutely unknown to him.

He was about to get into the pilot's seat when he saw, lying under a wing, the parachute that had evidently been dropped by the rightful pilot of the machine. Having no definite purpose in mind, but neglecting no precaution, he put it on, and then got into his seat. The watch on the instrument board told him that it was now nearly three o'clock.

It began to snow just as he took off, not the small driving flakes of a blizzard, but big, heavy flakes that dropped like white feathers straight down from the darkening sky. He might well have cursed it, but knowing that this could serve no useful purpose, he merely regarded it with thoughtful brooding eyes.

In a minute he was in the air, roaring eastward, keeping low so that he could watch the ground, for once he lost it he might have a job to find it again – without colliding violently with it. Thicker fell the snow as the minutes passed, and by the time he was halfway back to the fort the ground was no more than a dark grey blur. Still he roared on, hoping for the best. There was nothing else he could do. But the snow fell even more thickly, until it seemed that the heavens were emptying themselves over the desolate land.

He was down to a hundred feet when he got back over the aerodrome; he could just see the giant hangars and the hill that rose behind them. He cleared the fort by only a few feet.

The position now seemed hopeless, for he knew that once he lost touch with the aerodrome he would be utterly lost, and landing would be a matter of extreme danger. He had one stroke of luck. It seemed that the ground staff at the aerodrome had been alert, and assuming that the machine would want to land, they had turned the beam of a searchlight into the sky, and to this Biggles clung as a drowning man clings to a plank. Yet to land on the aerodrome was out of the question, for the second he was down the mechanics would be certain to run out to him, when he would instantly be discovered. Desperately he racked his brain for a solution to the problem. He could think of only one, and that was not one that would have appealed to him in the ordinary way. However, his plight was so desperate that he was in no position to choose.

Turning the bomber, he headed back towards the beam, at the same time climbing up to a thousand feet. The earth of course had disappeared; all he could see was the beam, and that only faintly. With professional skill he adjusted the elevators so that the machine would fly 'hands off' on even keel; and opening the emergency tool kit under the seat, he took from it a file and a pair of pliers, which he thrust into his jacket pocket. Then he opened the door, and when he judged that he was over the fort, he launched himself into space. Instinctively he counted the regulation 'one – two – three' and then pulled the ripcord.

He had made many parachute jumps, but none like this. He could see nothing; he could feel nothing except the harness taut round his limbs, telling him that the brolly had opened. All he could hear was the drone of the bomber as it ploughed on untended through the murk. One thing only he had in his favour – there was no wind. A dark mass loomed below him. Bending his knees and folding his arms over his face, he waited for the shock.

When it came he fell headlong, clutching wildly at anything he could catch, while the billowing folds of the fabric settled over him. Apart from being slightly winded by the impact he was unhurt, for which he was truly thankful, for a broken bone, or even a sprain, would have been fatal to his project. Throwing the fabric impatiently to one side, he slipped out of the harness and looked about him. To his intense satisfaction he saw that his judgement had been correct – or nearly so. He had hoped to drop into the courtyard, but instead, he had landed on the ramparts, which suited him even better, for these ramparts were, in fact, actually the flat roof over the occupied part of the fort.

In order that his position should be understood precisely, a brief description of the fort, as seen from above, becomes necessary. Like many military buildings of the late medieval period, it took the form of a hollow square. That is to say, the buildings, instead of being constructed in a solid block, were built round a central courtyard of about an acre of ground, which served the garrison as a parade ground. In other words, the buildings were really a fortified wall in the form of a square with a parapet on the outside. It was on the top of this wall that he had landed, so that a sheer drop occurred on both sides. On one hand was the outside of the fort; on the inside, the parade ground.

On this wall the snow had, of course, settled, and he examined it quickly, for footmarks would suggest that it was patrolled by a sentry; however, he found none. Then, suddenly, the snow turned to sleet, and then to rain, big heavy drops that hissed softly into the white mantle that lay over everything.

'Snow – sleet – rain – there isn't much else it can do,' he told himself philosophically, crouching low as he surveyed the scene in order to locate the room in which the others were confined – unless they had been moved. This was no easy matter, for by now it was practically dark; still, the darkness served one useful purpose in that it would hide him from the eyes of anyone who happened to cross the courtyard.

The room in which they had been locked was on the inside of the rampart wall; that he knew, for the window overlooked the courtyard. From it that morning he had remarked a well, and this now gave him a line on the position of the window he was anxious to find. Rolling the parachute into a ball, he put it under his arm and made his way cautiously towards his objective. Presently he was able to see that only one window was barred, and that told him all he wanted to know. But a new difficulty now presented itself. The window was a good six feet below the coping, and except for a narrow sill, there was nothing, no projection of any sort, by which he might descend to it. The solution of this problem was at hand, however; twisting the parachute's shrouds into a skein, he wound the fabric round one of the projecting battlements, made it secure, and then lowered the shrouds so that they hung in front of the window. In another moment his feet were on the sill. Bending, he looked in through the window.

CHAPTER VI

Biggles Comes Back

After Biggles had gone the feelings of the others can be better imagined than described. Their confidence in their leader was tremendous, but they could not deceive themselves, and without discussing it they knew in their hearts that the task with which he was now faced, the recovery of the papers and their escape from the fort, was, on the face of it, so tremendous that it seemed fantastic even to contemplate it. So they passed a miserable day; they saw it start snowing, and were glad when darkness began to envelop the gloomy scene outside. What had become of Biggles they did not so much as conjecture, knowing it to be futile.

'He'll turn up,' remarked Ginger confidently. 'I don't know how he manages it, but he always does.' He started violently, peering forward in the direction of the window. 'Great Scott!' he went on. 'Can you see what I see, or am I going crazy?' His voice was so high pitched that it bordered on the hysterical.

The others both stared at the window. Neither of them spoke. Algy got up from the bed on which he had been sitting, and walked, a step at a time, towards the window. 'It's Biggles,' he said in a funny voice. 'If it isn't, then it's his ghost.' He seemed bewildered, which is hardly a matter for wonder, for even if Biggles had escaped and returned to the fort, which seemed unlikely enough in all conscience, Algy could not imagine how, without wings, he had got to the window, for below there was a sheer drop of thirty feet. He reached the window just as Biggles tapped on it sharply with the file, which he had taken from his pocket.

Algy opened the window, which was only fastened by a simple latch, the frames opening inwards because of the bars. 'So here you are,' he said in a dazed voice. It seemed a silly thing to say, but he could think of nothing else.

'As you remark, here I am,' answered Biggles cheerfully. 'Now listen. Here's a file. One of you stay near the door so that you aren't caught in the act, while the others get to work on these bars. You'll have to cut one of them clean out. It's half-inch iron, but it should be fairly soft and shouldn't take you more than an hour. I daren't stay here in case anyone comes into the courtyard and looks up, so I'm going back on the ramparts. I shall stay handy, so as soon as you're through give a low whistle. There's no time for explanations now.'

'Okay,' agreed Algy eagerly, and took the file, while Biggles's dangling legs disappeared upward as he dragged himself back to the ramparts.

The others had all heard what Biggles had said, so there was no need to waste time in bartering words. Ginger went to the door, while Smyth, who was the handiest man with a file, set to work on the centre bar. He went at it with a will, and the steel fairly bit into the rusty iron.

Biggles squatted on the ramparts in no small discomfort, for it was bitterly cold and he had no protection from the rain. However, there was nothing he could do except blow on his hands to prevent them from becoming numb, as he listened to the file rasping into the iron. In this way nearly an hour passed. Nothing happened to interrupt the work. Occasional sounds below suggested that guards were being changed, but no sentry came to the ramparts.

Biggles lay down and peered over the edge of the wall. 'How are you getting on?' he whispered hoarsely.

'Fine! We're through the bottom and nearly through the top. Ten minutes should do it,' answered Algy.

Biggles lay still, waiting. The filing ceased. A moment later there was a soft snap as the iron parted.

'We're through,' came Algy's voice. 'How do we get up?'

'I'll lower a rope,' answered Biggles. 'It's a bunch of parachute shrouds. Grab the lot and I'll pull you up. It's no use going down into the courtyard because we may not be able to get out. We've got to get down the *outside* of the wall. As far as I can see it's about thirty feet, and ends on some rocks.'

In a few minutes they were all on the ramparts; Algy was last up, having closed the window behind him. 'I'd like to see von Stalhein's face when he calls and finds the room empty,' he chuckled.

'Let's save the laughter until we're the other side of the frontier,' suggested Biggles. 'I've got those confounded papers on me and they give me the heebie-jeebies. I'm scared stiff at the thought of being caught with them.'

'Where did you get this brolly?'

'Borrowed it,' returned Biggles tersely, as he pulled up the shrouds and lowered them again on the outer side of the ramparts. He peered down, but although the rain had nearly stopped, it was too dark to see anything distinctly. 'You'd better go first Algy,' he said. 'Let us know if it's all clear.'

Algy took the shrouds in a bundle in his hands, and forcing his feet against the wall in the manner of a rock climber, went down backwards. His voice, low and vibrant, floated up: 'All right – come on.'

The others descended in turn, and found themselves on a narrow ledge about a hundred feet above the village. The ledge appeared to follow the walls of the fort, but there were several places where a descent was possible.

'What about the brolly?' asked Ginger. It was still hanging on the wall.

'Leave it where it is,' decided Biggles. 'It's too bulky to carry about and I don't think we shall need it again. It won't be seen until it gets light, and by that time we ought to be clear away.'

After scrambling down the rock to the level ground below, Biggles instinctively headed for the hangars, hoping to find an aircraft outside, but, no doubt on account of the weather, they had all been taken in. What was even more disturbing, there seemed to be a good deal of activity; lights glowed dimly through the canvas walls of the hangars, and men, singly and in parties, moved about them. Biggles backed away into the shadows.

'It's going to be a dangerous business trying to get one of these kites,' he muttered anxiously. 'They're all big machines – too big for just the four of us to handle on the ground. The ground staff here use tractors to haul them about – I've heard them. It's difficult—'

'Gosh! It's a long walk home if that's what you're thinking,' whispered Ginger.

'It must be getting on for fifty miles to the lake where I crashed the Blenheim, and then a fair distance to the frontier.' Biggles seemed to be speaking his thoughts aloud.

'We should never make it without grub,' declared Algy.

'There's food in the Blenheim.'

'But that's nearly fifty miles away!'

'Still, it would help us on our way if we could get to it. We've got to try. As far as I can see we've no choice.'

They crouched back from the narrow track that passed behind the hangars as a sound could be heard approaching. Presently a sledge drawn by a pony went past.

'By Jove! If we could get hold of that,' whispered Algy.

'We'll follow it,' decided Biggles instantly. 'It's ten to one that it will stop in the village, and the fellow may leave it to make a call.'

Keeping at a safe distance, they followed the sledge to the outskirts of the village, where, as Biggles had predicted, the driver stopped outside a house; boisterous conversation and the clinking of glasses suggested that it was a tavern. Leaving the vehicle, the driver went in. Yellow light flashed on the road as he opened the door, and was cut off again as it closed behind him.

'Stay here!' Biggles's voice was crisp. He glanced quickly up and down the road; there was nobody about. Walking quietly up to the pony, he took the bridle in his hand and led the animal back to where the others were standing. 'The next thing is to get on the lake,' he announced. 'If we can do that we can make a bee-line due west.'

It took them some minutes before they found a lane descending to the lakeside. On the way they had to pass several houses, or rather hovels, and they had a bad moment when the door of one of them opened and a man came out. However, he appeared to see nothing unusual in the sledge, for he said nothing, and disappeared into the gloom in the direction of the tavern.

As soon as they were on the ice Biggles climbed into the driver's seat. 'Get aboard,' he ordered, and the others scrambled up on what turned out to be a load of hay. Biggles took a bearing from the stars, which here and there flickered mistily through breaks in the clouds, and shook the reins. The pony walked a few paces and then broke into a trot.

What none of them expected, having had no experience of this mode of travel, was the noise made by the sledge-runners on the ice. They hummed like circular saws as they cut through the layer of rain-softened snow into the hard ice underneath, and Biggles looked apprehensively in the direction of the hangars, which were only about a hundred yards away. However, having started there was no going back, and he drew a deep breath of relief as the lights gradually faded into the darkness behind them. He realised that the snow was both a blessing and a curse, for while it gave grip to the pony's hooves, it marked a track that could not be missed. All around lay a flat, seemingly endless expanse of greyish snow, with coal-black patches of sheer ice where, for some reason not apparent, the snow had melted. Such patches were as slippery as glass, as Biggles soon discovered when the pony ran on the first one and nearly fell, so thereafter he avoided them. He called Algy up beside him, and as he did so a searchlight stabbed the sky behind them. For a moment it flung its beam towards the stars; then it swooped swiftly down and began playing on the ice, sweeping the surface like a white sword.

'What does that mean?' asked Algy sharply.

'I imagine it means that our escape has been discovered,' replied Biggles quietly. 'The owner of the sledge may have missed it, or the Commandant of the fort has discovered the room empty. The hunt is on.'

'They'll spot our tracks, even if they don't see us.'

'I'm afraid you're right.'

'Shouldn't we abandon the sledge?'

'Not yet – this is a lot better than walking.'

As he spoke, Biggles flicked the pony with the whip; it broke into a gallop, and they went flying over the ice with the runners fairly singing. Twice the searchlight nearly caught them in its dazzling beam, but, as if it sensed the danger, the pony tore on, and soon they were beyond the reach of the blinding radiance, a tiny black speck in a world of utter desolation.

'How wide is this lake?' asked Algy.

'I don't know exactly, but from what I saw of it from the plane this morning it must be pretty wide – not less than forty miles I reckon. We've got to be off it before dawn, though, or those bombers will be on us like a ton of bricks. They'd be bound to see us, when they could please themselves whether they landed and picked us up, or just bombed the ice so that we fell in.'

'Gosh,' muttered Algy, 'what a cheerful bloke you are!'

'The clouds are our salvation so far,' resumed Biggles. 'They make it just too dark for safe flying. The moment they go it will start to get lighter. What we really want is a spot of snow to keep the bombers out of the air.'

'What I want,' returned Algy bitingly, 'is a hot drink and a fur coat. Jumping rattlesnakes! Isn't it cold?'

'We've got to stick it for a bit,' Biggles told him. 'When we get to the other side and start running we shall be warm enough. We shall have to watch out that we don't bump into von Stalhein. I left him out here this morning with a bunch of Russians, but I fancy he's a bit to the north of us.' Biggles gave the others a brief account of his adventures earlier in the day, and after that they fell silent. The pony, tiring, steadied its pace. The only sound was the hollow thud of its hooves and the whine of the runners on the ice. Ginger and Smyth, deep down in the hay, dozed uneasily. Biggles, his face expressionless, stared into the gloom ahead.

CHAPTER VII

The Avalanche

Dawn saw the rim of a hazy red sun peeping over the horizon behind them, throwing a strange pinky glow over the flat surface of the lake. After the darkness it was a relief to have the light, for it enabled the weary travellers to see where they were, although Biggles several times looked anxiously to the rear.

They could now see the edge of the lake in two directions, to the north and to the west, in which direction they were moving – moving slowly, for the pony was near the end of its endurance. To the north the land showed as low, snow-covered hills. Ahead, at a distance of perhaps four miles, a barrier of steeper hills rose sharply and formed a jagged skyline, with dark patches of rock showing where the rain had washed away the snow. Sweeping forests of spruce and fir, which had also shed much of their white mantle, could be seen.

Biggles urged the pony on, not without a qualm of conscience, for it had proved a willing little beast and had served them well; but out on the ice as they were, he knew that they were as conspicuous as a fly on a white ceiling. Once they reached the trees they would find cover, both from above and from the surrounding country, so that was the first consideration. Gradually the forest for which Biggles was heading drew nearer, but the pace had dropped to a walk, for the pony could obviously do no more. Twice aircraft could be heard behind them, and Biggles wondered why the pilots did not strike the trail and follow it – until Ginger called attention to what none of them had noticed; a sharp thaw had set in, causing the snow to start melting, and thus obliterate the trail except for a short distance behind them. Indeed, the snow was now soft and slushy, and as soon as he realised it Biggles got down, made the others do the same, and ran beside the sledge. Relieved of their weight, the pony put on a spurt, and reached the edge of the lake just as a bomber appeared in the distance.

Biggles led the stout little animal in amongst the trees where he thought they would be safe, unharnessed it, and flung the hay out on the snow. 'There you are, laddie,' he said, patting its neck. 'That ought to keep you going till the snow melts.'

He insisted on remaining under cover until the bomber, whose circling progress left them in no doubt as to its mission, passed on; then he turned to the ridge of hills which, running from north to south, lay across their path. 'This is where we start walking,' he announced.

'D'you know where we are?' inquired Ginger.

'No, but as long as we keep heading westwards we ought to be all right. From the ridge in front of us we should be able to see the lake where we crashed the Blenheim. I made a note of it yesterday from the air. I'm aiming to strike the Blenheim in order to pick up some food.'

The climb up the steep, snow-covered slope was a severe one, particularly as the thaw was now perceptible; indeed, after the intense cold the air seemed muggy, and they were soon perspiring freely. A steamy mist began to form.

'Phew, take it easy,' muttered Algy, taking off his jacket and sitting down on a rock to rest. 'There's no need for us to break our necks.'

Biggles agreed, so they all took off their jackets and sat on them while they got their breath preparatory to tackling the last climb, which, as is usually the case, was the hardest part. Refreshed, with their jackets over their arms, they went on, and after a sharp tussle reached the top.

Biggles was first on the ridge; he gave a cry and pointed triumphantly, for the ground fell away again to another lake, and there, no great distance away, lay the twisted remains of the Blenheim. Sliding and slipping, and sometimes jumping over difficult places, they hurried on down the steep bank towards the ice, anxious to secure the food which they hoped was still in the Blenheim.

Suddenly Biggles remembered something; in fact, it was a patch of loose snow that slid away under his feet that recalled to his mind what he had often heard, but of which he had so far had no personal experience – that a sharp thaw is liable to cause an avalanche. 'Steady!' he cried urgently. 'Steady, everybody.' When first he spoke he only sensed the danger, but now he saw it, for in several places the snow was beginning to slide. Unfortunately Algy was poised on an awkward-shaped piece of rock; he slipped, and to save himself he jumped clear.

'Stop!' yelled Biggles – but it was too late.

Slowly at first, but with ever increasing momentum, the whole slope on which they were standing started to slide, and once started there was no stopping it. Biggles did not waste time trying to stop it. 'Run!' he shouted, and began running sideways along the slope to get clear of the danger area.

The others looked up, and went deathly white as, too late, they realised what was happening. With a mighty roar a thousand tons of snow and rock broke loose. Tearing up trees as if they had been so much brushwood, the mass thundered down the slope towards the ice.

Now it happened that Biggles was some distance to the right of the others and, naturally, he took what appeared to be the shortest cut to safety. The others went in the opposite direction – anywhere to escape the awful thing that was happening. In their wild rush they took the most desperate chances, jumping over obstacles which in the ordinary way would have made them pause. Algy practically got clear. So did Smyth, although he was bowled over. For a moment it seemed that Ginger, too, might escape the terrifying wave of death that was roaring down the slope. But he was outflanked; he had been nearest to Biggles and consequently had farther to go. Caught in the fringe of the tumbling mass, in a flash he was whirled away. For a moment Algy and Smyth could see him rolling over and over amongst the snow; then he disappeared from sight.

Algy stared like a man stunned, gazing blankly at the confused jumble of snow, ice, rock, and timber as the avalanche swept past them, swirling and tossing like water in a ravine flooded by a cloudburst. Dimly he was conscious of a great noise without actually hearing it. He reeled under the suddenness of the calamity. The scene was engraved on his mind like a photograph.

Slowly the avalanche exhausted itself, the lip far out on the ice. Silence fell. Snow which had been flung high into the air began to fall silently on the bare bedrock.

Algy turned a stricken face to the side of the slope where he had last seen Biggles. There was no sign of him. Nor could he see Ginger. He turned to Smyth. 'We'd better look for them,' he said in a hopeless sort of voice. 'You try to find Ginger – I'll look for the Skipper.'

Before he had reached the place where Biggles had disappeared Smyth was yelling to him to come back. Shaking like a leaf from shock, he hurried to the spot, to find Smyth clawing frantically at a great pile of loose snow from which projected a leg. It took them only a few minutes to drag Ginger clear. He was unconscious and bleeding from the nose, but a quick examination revealed no broken bones.

'We shall have to leave him where he is for the moment,' muttered Algy. 'Let's see if we can find the Skipper.'

They made their way over the lacerated ground to where Biggles had last been seen.

For some minutes they hunted in vain, and then Smyth saw him. Either he had just escaped the avalanche and then fallen, or had been overwhelmed by it and flung clear, for he lay motionless, face downwards, among the debris of rocks and uprooted trees which had surged far out on the ice of the lake. Half sick with dread, Algy turned him over and got him into as comfortable a position as could be arranged. He was unconscious.

Algy caught his breath when he saw a livid bruise, seeping blood, on the ashen forehead. 'My God! That looks like concussion,' he whispered through lips that were as white as Biggles's. 'This is awful. What are we going to do? We've got to get him off the ice, both of them, or they'll die of sheer cold.'

Algy spoke in a dazed voice. He was, in fact, half stunned by the shock of the catastrophe. Their position had been difficult enough before, but now, with two casualties on their hands, it seemed hopeless, and he was in a fever of dismay. The ghastly part of it was that there was so little they could do.

As they stood staring down at Biggles's unconscious form a weak hail made them look up, to see Ginger reeling down the hill.

'Stand still, you fool!' yelled Algy. 'You'll fall and break your neck.' He raced up the hill, for the warning went unheeded. He caught Ginger and dragged him back from the edge of a steep rock on which he was staggering, and forced him to sit down.

'Did Biggles – get clear?' asked Ginger weakly.

'Yes, but he's knocked out. How do you feel?'

Ginger shut his eyes and shook his head. 'I don't know,' he muttered. 'My legs are a bit groggy – but I don't think I've done myself – any real – damage. Great Scott! What a dreadful mess.'

Smyth came up. 'We'd better get them under cover, sir, until we see how badly the Skipper's hurt,' he said seriously.

'Under cover?'

Smyth pointed to the fuselage of the Blenheim lying flat on the ice. 'Let's get them inside,' he suggested. 'That will be better than lying out here. Otherwise they're liable to freeze, particularly as the Skipper hasn't got a jacket. He was carrying it, wasn't he? I wonder what happened to it.'

Algy looked around. 'I don't see it,' he said dully. 'I suppose it's buried under all this snow. Well, we haven't time to look for it now – we'll get them into the

Blenheim. Now I come to think of it, there's a first-aid outfit there – or there should be.'

They helped Ginger out onto the smooth ice, where they found that he was able to walk unaided, although, in spite of his assurances to the contrary, it was obvious that he had been badly shaken, if nothing worse. Biggles was still unconscious, and as he was a difficult load on the slippery ice, they made a rough bed of fir branches and, taking the thick ends in their hands, began to drag him towards the Blenheim.

They were just about halfway, in the most open part of the lake, when, faintly at first, but developing swiftly, came the roar of an aircraft; and the beat of the engines told them what it was even before it came into view – a Russian heavy bomber. Algy, realising how conspicuous they were, threw up his hands in dismay. 'We're sunk,' he cried bitterly.

'Algy!'

Algy started as if he had been stung, for the word came from the improvised stretcher. He saw that Biggles's eyes were open.

'Listen,' went on Biggles. 'Do exactly as I tell you. There's a gun in my hip pocket – get it out. You've no time to get under cover, so lie down, all of you, as if you were dead. Don't move a muscle. There's just a chance that if the pilot spots you he'll land to see what's happened. If he does, stick him up and grab the machine. It's our only chance.' Biggles tried to get up, but his face twisted with pain and he fell back again. His eyes closed.

It took Algy only a moment to secure the pistol. 'You heard what he said,' he told the others tersely. 'Lie down and don't move.'

They all collapsed on the ice just as the bomber swept over the trees. The pilot saw them at once, as he was bound to, and Algy, whose eyes remained open, watched the movements of the machine with breathless suspense.

Three times the bomber circled, coming lower each time; the third time his wheels nearly brushed them. A white face, fur-rimmed, evidently that of the second pilot, projected from the cockpit and stared down from a height of not more than twenty feet. The bomber went on, reached the end of the lake, turned, and then, cutting its engines, glided back, obviously with the intention of landing.

'Don't move, anybody,' hissed Algy. 'Wait till I give the word.'

The bomber's wheels rumbled as they kissed the ice, and the massive undercarriage groaned as they trundled on, the machine finishing its run about fifty yards from the fugitives. There was a brief delay; then a door in the cockpit opened, and two men descended and began walking quickly over the ice towards the bodies. Algy's nerves tingled as their footsteps drew nearer. He half closed his eyes.

The Russians were talking in low tones, evidently discussing the situation. Then one of them must have noticed the avalanche, for he pointed to it. They both stopped, held a brief discussion, and then came on again. In short, their reaction to the situation was perfectly natural. There was no reason for them to suppose that they were walking into a trap.

To his joy Algy saw that neither of them carried a weapon; their hands were empty – except that one care-lessly swung his gauntlets. They went first to Biggles. The leading pilot knelt to examine him while his companion looked on, a position in which their backs were turned to the others.

Very quietly Algy stood up, pistol at the ready. 'Don't move,' he said curtly.

It is unlikely that the Russians understood English, but they knew the meaning of the squat black weapon that menaced them, for the message it conveys is universal. Their eyes opened wide in amazement. Slowly they raised their hands.

As Ginger and Smyth joined the party Algy stepped nearer to the two Russians and tapped their pockets; then, satisfied that they were unarmed, he indicated that they were to start walking towards the bank. A pilot himself, he felt a certain sympathy for them, and realising that they had a long walk in front of them before they could get home, he pointed first to the crash and then to his mouth in the hope that they would grasp what he was trying to convey – that there was food to be found there.

The Russians looked at each other, and then back at Algy. One nodded; the other waved his hand in a manner that suggested that he understood.

All the same, Algy watched them as they walked on, while Ginger and Smyth got Biggles to the bomber and lifted him inside. They called out that they were ready.

Algy hastened to join them. The engines were still ticking over. He climbed into the pilot's seat and slammed the door. His hand closed over the throttle. 'We're away!' he cried jubilantly.

The propellers swirled as he opened the throttle and turned the machine to face the longest run that the lake provided. His eyes explored the surface of the ice, for he didn't want a repetition of the Blenheim disaster; but there were no obstructions. The engines bellowed. The bomber surged forward; its tail lifted, and in a minute it was in the air heading westwards.

Grinning all over his face, Ginger joined Algy in the cockpit. 'This,' he declared cheerfully, 'is something like it. We ought to be home in a couple of hours.'

Algy nodded, but without enthusiasm, for he was still a trifle worried. He was wondering what would happen when they came to the Finnish anti-aircraft batteries.

CHAPTER VIII

A Bitter Blow

Algy breathed a sigh of relief when they roared across the frontier, for now, he thought, if the worst came to the worst, they could at least land with reasonable promise of security. In his heart he was aware that he was taking a risk in remaining in the air, and that in order to be quite safe he ought to land, perhaps near an outlying homestead where they could lie snug until a relief party came for them. Yet every minute they remained in the air took them three miles nearer home, and the temptation to fly on and get as near to their base as possible was irresistible. He flew with one hand on the throttle, every nerve alert; not for a moment did he abandon his attentive scrutiny of the sky or the white landscape that flashed underneath.

Ahead lay a wide bank of indigo cloud, and he eyed it suspiciously, only too well aware of the perils that might lurk in it, for in war, unless he is driven into them by force of circumstances, a wise airman gives clouds a wide berth; they provide cover for prowling scouts. He was now within a hundred miles of home and his common sense warned him to take no chances, so he decided to run under the cloud and then land at the first reasonable landing-ground that he could find, preferably one near a house or village.

He left it just a minute too long. Where the Gladiator came from he did not see; but a wild yell broke from Ginger, and simultaneously a slim grey shape carrying Finnish markings seemed to materialise out of nothing. In a flash the Gladiator was on him, its guns rattling like demoniac castanets.

Algy flicked back the throttle and made for the ground; he would have done so in any case, but he spotted the number 13 painted on the Gladiator's nose, and he knew the man to whom it belonged – Eddie Hardwell, an American volunteer from their own aerodrome, and perhaps one of the most deadly fighter pilots on the front. He had already shot down five Russian bombers.

Ginger, too, saw the number, and threw up his hands in impotence, for although he had a gun he could not, of course, use it.

The Gladiator's first burst made a colander of the bomber's tail; it swept up and past in a beautiful climbing turn, and then came back, a spitting fury.

Ginger's presence of mind saved the situation. He knew that this time the Gladiator would rake them from prop-boss to tailskid, in which case only a miracle could preserve them. Breathless from suspense, he climbed out on a wing, scrambled onto the back of the great fuselage, and raised his hands in the air in an attitude of surrender.

The fighter pilot swerved, suspecting a trick, but as no gun was brought to bear on him he flew closer and, leaning out of his cockpit, jabbed his hand downwards in an unmistakable signal that the bomber was to land.

Algy did not need telling to go down; he was already going down as fast as safety permitted. He had half a dozen lakes to choose from, for from the centre to the southern end of Finland there is as much water as land. He chose the largest, and as soon as he saw that he was in a satisfactory position for landing he switched off his engines to prove to Hardwell that he was in earnest. A minute later the bomber was trundling over the ice.

The Gladiator circled it once or twice while the occupants, with the exception of Biggles, got out and stood with their hands up. After that the Gladiator made a pretty landing. Revolver in hand, the pilot climbed down and walked over to the party. Suddenly he stopped dead. He blinked, passed his hand over his eyes and looked again.

'Suff'rin' coyotes!' he cried. 'What's the big idea?'

'Easy with the gun, Eddie,' returned Algy. 'We're all here.'

The American put the revolver in his pocket and came on. 'You guys are sure aimin' ter spill yerselves over the landscape, barnstorming in that Rusky pantechnicon. What's the racket?'

'No racket, Eddie. We crashed our Blenheim the wrong side of the frontier, and borrowed this kite to get home in.'

'Okay – I get it.'

'What are you doing around here, anyway? It isn't your usual beat,' inquired Algy.

'I was looking for you,' replied Eddie surprisingly.

'Looking for us?' Algy was incredulous.

'Yeah. There's a guy arrived from England asking for you. We told him you hadn't come back, which seemed to upset him, but he asked one or two of us to have a look round to see if we could spot you. The guy he was most anxious to find seemed to be Bigglesworth. Where is he?'

'He's inside. He got knocked about a bit. What was the name of this fellow from England, did he say?'

'Sure – said his name was Raymond.'

Algy gasped. 'Great Scott! Look, Eddie, this is serious,' he said confidentially. 'We've been on a special mission – to get something for Raymond. He's one of the heads of British Intelligence. Well, we've got what we went for, and he ought to know about it right away. Will you do us a favour?'

'Sure.'

'Then fly back to Oskar, get hold of Raymond and tell him that we're here. At the same time you might ask somebody to fly out in a Blenheim and fetch us home.'

'Okay, buddy; I'll get right along.'

Eddie returned to his machine. It raced across the ice, swept into the air and nosed its way into the western sky. In a minute it was out of sight.

The others returned to the bomber. Ginger was now practically normal, but Biggles was still in a bad way, and seemed only semi-conscious. The others did what they could to make him comfortable. Some peasants, seeing the Finnish uniforms, went off and came back with a doctor. A woman brought a can of hot soup.

The doctor examined Biggles thoroughly, and finally announced that apart from the blow on the head he was suffering only from shock. At least, no bones were broken. The blow on the head had been a severe one, and had it not been for the fact that Biggles's skull was exceptionally hard, it would certainly have been fractured. He dressed the wound, bandaged it, and gave the patient a pick-me-up. The effect of this, followed by a bowl of soup, was instantly apparent, and Biggles's condition improved visibly. In two hours he was able to sit up and announce that, except for a splitting headache, he was all right.

It was at this moment that the roar of aircraft over-head announced the arrival of the relief party – Eddie's

Gladiator followed by a Blenheim. Eddie, it transpired, had come back to show the Blenheim just where the Russian bomber had landed. In a few minutes Colonel Raymond could be seen walking over the ice. He nodded a greeting to Algy, but was too perturbed for conventional pleasantries. He went straight to Biggles.

'Are you all right?' he asked quickly.

Biggles smiled wanly. 'Not so bad,' he answered. 'Silly, wasn't it, giving myself a crack on the nut just as the show was practically over. It was a sticky business, too, largely as a result of running into our old friend von Stalhein.'

Colonel Raymond started. 'What! Is *he* here?'

'Too true he is.'

'Then those papers must be even more important than we at first supposed. Did you get them?'

'Of course – otherwise we shouldn't have come back.'

'Where are they?'

Biggles held out his hand to Algy. 'Give me my jacket, laddie, will you.'

Algy looked puzzled. A strange look came into his eyes. 'Your jacket – yes – of course. I – er – well, that is – Ginger, where did you put Biggles's jacket?'

Ginger looked round the cabin, then back at Algy. 'Jacket?' he echoed foolishly. 'Now you mention it, I don't remember seeing it.'

An awful look came over Biggles's face. He staggered to his feet, glaring at Algy. 'Did you come back here without my jacket?' He spoke slowly, in a curiously calm voice.

Algy had turned pale. 'I – I suppose we must have done,' he faltered.

Biggles sank back like a man whose legs will no longer support him.

'I remember now,' resumed Algy. 'You see, after the avalanche we were too concerned about getting you to the Blenheim to bother about your jacket. I remember looking for it, but it didn't seem to be about, so – well, we didn't bother any more about it.' In a few words he described what had happened. 'After all, I didn't know the papers were in your jacket pocket, although I suppose I might have guessed it,' he concluded.

'It was muggy, and we were carrying our jackets over our arms when the avalanche hit us,' Biggles told Colonel Raymond bitterly. 'I shouldn't have taken my jacket off, of course, but how the dickens was I to know that we were going to get smothered under a perishing landslide?'

The Colonel's face expressed disappointment, but he was too much of a soldier to waste time in useless recriminations. He spoke to Algy. 'You say you couldn't see the coat after the avalanche?'

'No, sir. Had it been there I could hardly have failed to see it.'

'Then it comes to this. The jacket must be still there, buried under the snow.'

'I don't think there's any doubt about that,' answered Biggles gloomily. Then, suddenly, he laughed. 'Forgive me,' he implored the Colonel, 'I can't help it. It's the daftest thing I ever did or ever heard of. If you only knew what we went through to get those confounded documents – and now we rush back home and leave them lying in the snow like a lot of waste paper. You must admit it has its funny side.'

Colonel Raymond looked doubtful.

'It's all right, Colonel – don't worry; I'll slip back and fetch them,' promised Biggles.

'Oh, no, you won't. I'll go,' declared Algy.

'Better let me go,' put in Ginger. 'I know exactly where Biggles was lying, and the jacket can't be far away.'

Biggles raised his hand. 'When you've all finished arguing maybe you'll remember who's in charge of this flight,' he said curtly. 'We've got to get the papers – there's no question about that. The thing, then, is to find the most expeditious way of getting them, and I've already decided that. For reasons which I needn't go into it would be unwise to go back in this machine. In any case, it would be foolish for all of us to go back in *any* machine. We four are the only people who know where the papers are, and if we were shot down or captured, the information would disappear with us. I'm going – alone. I'm going to borrow Eddie's Gladiator. With luck I ought to be back in a couple of hours, although that depends, of course, on how long it takes me to find the jacket. The rest of you will go home, get some food inside you and have a good night's rest. If I'm not back at Oskar by this time tomorrow you can reckon that something's gone wrong. Then one of you can have a go – but don't go together. Toss up for it – that's the fairest way. If number two fails to return, then number three goes. If he fails, then number four gets his chance. One of us ought to succeed. If we all go west, then we must be a pretty poor lot. That's the sane way of tackling it – don't you agree, Colonel?'

Colonel Raymond smiled lugubriously. 'Yes,' he said, 'I think it is; it's certainly wiser than putting all our eggs in one basket. One stands just as much chance as four going together, so by going one at a time we quadruple our chances. The only thing that worries me, Bigglesworth, is this: are you fit to fly with your head in that state?'

'While I'm conscious I can fly,' declared Biggles grimly.

'All right; if you say so then it's not for me to say no. When are you going?'

'Right away,' returned Biggles promptly. He turned to Eddie, who had been listening to the conversation. 'D'you mind flying back in the Blenheim with the others, so that I can have your machine?'

'Go right ahead,' agreed the American. 'But as I figger it, you guys have done enough for one day. What about letting me have a go at—'

'Hey, wait a minute, Eddie,' broke in Biggles. 'That's very kind of you and we all appreciate it, but this is our pigeon. Anyway, you don't know where the avalanche occurred, and it would take us a long time to describe the place even if we could, which I doubt.'

'Okay, buddy – but don't lose my kite if you can help it. You'd better have my leather coat, too.'

'I'll try to get the machine home in one piece,' promised Biggles.

'What are you going to take with you?' asked Algy.

'My gun and a couple of biscuits should be enough,' answered Biggles. 'I could do with a spade, in case I have to dig.'

'I should think one of these peasants would lend you a spade,' cut in the Colonel, indicating the men and women who had been slowly congregating on the ice to have a close look at the enemy bomber.

Inquiry soon produced the required implement, which Biggles stowed away in the Gladiator's fuselage. The others stood round while he got into his seat and fastened the safety belt. He waved his hand. 'See you later,' he called cheerfully.

The Gladiator roared across the ice like a blunt-nosed bullet, swept into the air and disappeared into the haze that hung in the eastern sky.

The others watched Biggles go with mixed feelings. They could not fail to see the wisdom of his plan, but none of them liked the idea of splitting up the party.

Colonel Raymond turned towards the Blenheim. 'I expect the Finns will take care of this Russian machine,' he said. 'Let's get back to Oskar. You all need a rest. Tonight you can tell me how you got hold of the papers.'

CHAPTER IX

'Grounded'

Biggles flew straight back to the lake on full throttle, for it was now mid-afternoon and he was anxious if possible to get back before dark. Naturally he kept a sharp lookout for hostile aircraft, but he had no fear of them, for alone in a highly manoeuvrable single-seater he felt well able to take care of himself whatever he might encounter in the air – with the possible exception of a formation of Messerschmitts, which, apart from being faster, were equipped with cannon. His head still ached and he felt tired, but the very urgency of his mission did much to allay his minor discomforts. As he flew he instinctively considered such contingencies as might possibly occur, in order that he might be prepared for them if they did. He saw one Russian bomber, far away to the south, near the north-eastern end of Lake Ladoga where fighting on the ground was in progress, but as he had a more pressing matter to attend to he ignored it, and soon afterwards it disappeared in an easterly direction.

There were many signs to indicate that the thaw had now properly set in; faces of rock were exposed where the snow had vanished, the trees showed darkly green, and the lakes, on which the thin coating of snow had disappeared, were as black as tar. This, he thought, would be to his advantage, for it meant that the snow that formed the avalanche would be diminishing, with the result that it would be easier for him to find the missing jacket. With luck it might even now be exposed, and so save him the labour of digging.

Reaching the lake, he made a swift reconnaissance, flying low over the wrecked Blenheim and circling the banks at a height that could not fail to reveal enemy troops if they were there. The lake, like the rest, was black, its sullen surface broken only by the remains of the crashed aircraft. There was not a movement anywhere. Satisfied that all was well, and reckoning now that the recovery of the jacket was only a matter of minutes, he lost no time in landing.

He had a shock when his wheels touched, for he was unprepared for the cloud of spray that shot into the air. Indeed, his alarm was such that he nearly took off again; but as the machine settled down he felt the hard ice under his tyres, so he allowed the Gladiator to run on. From the splash of the water and the speed with which it pulled him up, he judged that there could not be less than four inches of water on the ice, and this astounded him, for he could not understand how the ice had melted so quickly. Then, as the Gladiator stopped, seeming in some miraculous way to stand poised on water, he thought the thing out, and presently realised that it was not so much the melting ice that had produced the water, as water running down the banks and flooding it. Naturally, as the snow thawed it would run downhill and so flood the lake.

This was a contingency for which he had certainly not been prepared, and it rather worried him, for there seemed to be a risk of the ice melting and becoming too thin to support the weight of the machine before he could recover the jacket and get off it. Seriously concerned, he taxied up to the lip of the avalanche, where he jumped out and splashed through the icy water to the bank.

The scene that met his eyes appalled him. He had expected something pretty bad, but not as bad as he actually found, for now that much of the snow had disappeared the debris that remained, earth, rock, and trees, looked far worse than it had done originally. The snow that remained was dirty slush, through which trickled rivulets of water. He began to wonder if the papers would be any use even if he found them, and he could only hope that the varnished fabric in which they were wrapped would preserve them.

There was no sign of the jacket, but this did not surprise him, although he had hoped that it would now be exposed; moreover, he perceived that his chance of finding it by digging was not very bright, to say the best of it, for he had no idea whether the jacket had caught in some obstruction at the top of the hill, or whether it lay buried under the mass of rubbish at the bottom. There was this about it, however: the slush was fast melting, and the faster it went the easier his task would be – or so he thought.

He fetched the spade from the Gladiator and set to work exploring the chaos, not concentrating on any one spot, but making a general survey, and digging only round trees in the branches of which the jacket might have been caught. Darkness closed in, the gloomy twilight of northern latitudes, and finally compelled him to desist – at least, it made the search so difficult that it seemed hardly worth while going on with it, for not only would the jacket be hard to see, but there was a chance that he might slip in the mush and do himself an injury. Several times, as the snow that supported him gave way, rocks went plunging down the slope.

He lit a cigarette and for a minute or two gazed at the wild scene ruefully. He looked at the Gladiator; it was well in near the bank and there seemed little chance of its being seen from above. Still, he did not feel inclined to pass the night cramped up in the tiny cockpit. The big fuselage of the Blenheim looked more inviting, so he made his way to it, not without trepidation, for he found that walking over the invisible ice was disconcerting. However, he reached the machine and went inside, to find, as he expected, that the bottom of the fuselage was just high enough to be clear of the water. Nothing appeared to have been touched, so he made himself as comfortable as possible and prepared to wait for morning.

A more depressing spot would have been hard to find. Inside the cabin it was practically dark, and he dare not risk a light for fear it might be seen by a wandering enemy scout. All round lay the water, still, silent, black, and forbidding, with the sombre firs clustered like a frozen army on the sloping banks. His head ached. His feet were wet through, and consequently icy cold, and he had no means of drying them. There was this to be thankful for, though: everything inside the machine appeared to be exactly as it had been at the time of the crash, except that the food store had been depleted, presumably by the two Russian pilots. Still, there was more left than he was likely to require.

He was not in the mood for sleep. Indeed, he felt that it would be futile to try to sleep, so he sat in the seat under the centre gun-turret, occasionally smoking a cigarette, waiting for the dawn – a tedious way of passing a night at any time and in any place. Ultimately he must have dozed, for he was suddenly aware that the sky was turning grey. With a sigh of relief he stretched his cramped limbs, but then stiffened suddenly, staring aghast at the floor – or rather, the water that now covered it. Trial soon revealed the alarming fact that there was a good six inches of water in the cabin, and he realised instantly what this implied. The water over the whole lake had risen, and could not now be less than a foot deep.

For a moment he was staggered by the calamity, and wondered why he had not foreseen it. Cursing his stupidity, he prepared forthwith to evacuate his refuge and return to the Gladiator, which he could see standing just as he had left it, although it seemed to be lower in the water.

Cautiously he lowered himself onto the ice, and as he did so the full enormity of the disaster struck him for the first time, for the water came up to his knees. He did not mind that. What did upset him – to put it mildly – was the realisation that he would not be able to get the Gladiator into the air, for with such a depth of water dragging at its wheels it would not be able to achieve flying speed. The water, he knew, must be getting deeper every minute.

He made his way to the bank, which was a lot nearer than the Gladiator, for the prospect of wading knee-deep across the middle of the lake was not inviting. As it was, he walked with his heart in his mouth, for his weight was sufficient to cause the fast-melting ice to rock, and send tiny ripples surging towards the shore. He fully expected it to collapse at any moment and let him through. However, he reached the bank without mishap and set off at a run, following the edge of the lake towards the scene of the avalanche.

It took him nearly half an hour to reach it, or what was left of it, for the snow had nearly all disappeared. And then the first thing he saw was his jacket, tangled up in a small branch about fifty yards from the shore. The branch was sinking under the sodden weight of the garment, and he realised with a further shock that had he not arrived at that moment the papers would have been irretrievably lost. Quickly he waded out, dragged the jacket off the branch, and carried it back to the shore. The packet was still in his breast pocket, intact. 'Phew, that was a close thing,' he muttered, as he pushed the precious documents into the pocket of the flying jacket that he had borrowed from Eddie – the pocket in which he had found the cigarettes and matches.

There was nothing now to detain him, so he splashed out to the Gladiator, dragged himself, dripping, into the cockpit, and started the engine. In his heart he knew that he would never get the machine off the water, for its wheels were submerged, but he felt that he must try. He tried in vain. Up and down the lake he roared, cutting the water into a white, swirling wake, and in his anxiety taking the most desperate chances of turning a somersault. He saw that if he persisted in his efforts this was what would happen, with disastrous results. He made one last attempt, opening the throttle until the tail cocked high in the air, and the airscrew flipped up great clouds of spray; but the drag against the wheels was too much, and the machine was no more able to get up flying speed than if it had been in deep snow or soft sand – both equally fatal to an aeroplane. Reluctantly he taxied back to the bank, running the machine high and dry, and there he was compelled to abandon it, for it could be of no further service to him. As far as he knew there was not a level stretch of ground for miles, and even if there had been he had no means of getting the machine to it.

He prepared to walk home. There was nothing else for it. And he had, in fact, covered a hundred yards when a thought occurred to him, a thought so disturbing that he shook his head in dismay. For he saw that he dare not leave the lake. He would have to remain there, for this reason. When, in a few hours, he failed to turn up at Oskar one of the others would set out to look for him, and on arriving at the lake, probably not realising that it was now water instead of ice, would attempt to land on it, with a fatal result. From the air the motionless water would doubtless look like ice; he himself might well have made this same mistake had he not known what had happened. In the circumstances the only thing he could do was to remain where he was in order to warn Algy or Ginger, whichever of them came, that there could be no more landing on the lake. By the irony of fate, the very circumstance that had exposed his jacket now made it impossible for him to leave the place. There was this about it, he mused, as he hurried back to the Gladiator: whoever came would understand his plight and in some way attempt a rescue, although how this was to be achieved he could not imagine, for he knew of nowhere where an aircraft could land. A flying-boat or seaplane, or even an amphibian, would be able to get down on the water, but he had seen no such aircraft the whole time he had been in Finland, and did not even know if the Finns possessed such machines. There was certainly not one anywhere near Oskar.

Reaching the Gladiator, he took the signalling pistol from its pocket and, loading it with a red cartridge, prepared to wait. As a secondary precaution he gathered the driest twigs he could find. As soon as he heard the aircraft approaching he would light a fire; the pilot would see the smoke, and fly low over it to investigate before doing anything else. That would be the moment to fire the pistol. At the same time he could throw lumps of rock into the water, and the splash and the ripples would reveal it for what it was.

Having nothing more to do he climbed to the ridge above him, no great distance, from where he would be able to watch the western sky for the aircraft that should arrive some time during the afternoon.

He was relieved to see that the landscape was deserted, so there did not appear to be any immediate peril, for now that he again had the papers on his person he was filled with doubts and anxiety. Everywhere the snow was melting and water was gushing down to the lake; it was an ironical thought that, although the thaw was directly responsible for his present plight, had it not occurred he might never have found the papers. That, he ruminated, was always the way of things – the good luck balancing the bad.

Slowly the day wore on, and he looked forward to the time when he could discharge his obligation to whoever was on his way to the lake, so that he could start making his way home, for inactivity at any time is trying, but with wet feet it becomes irritating.

Then, suddenly, from a distance a sound reached his ears that brought him round with a start of alarm. It sounded like a shout or a laugh. At first he could see nobody; then, surprisingly, dangerously close, he saw a column of men marching over the brow of a hill that had previously hidden them from view. They were Russian soldiers, and they were making straight towards the lake.

CHAPTER X

Awkward Predicaments

Biggles sank down so that he could not be seen and stared at the Russians in something like dismay, for their presence put an entirely new complexion on the whole situation. It was obvious that they were making for the lake, and a number of sledges suggested that they were likely to stay for some time. He suspected – correctly, as it presently transpired – that it was a salvage party coming to collect the contents of the Blenheim, or such component parts as were worth saving.

Biggles tried to sort out the hundred and one thoughts that rushed into his mind, and the first was, what was he himself going to do? The Russians were unaware of his presence; there was no reason for them even to suspect that he might be there, and in the ordinary way he would have had no difficulty in keeping them in ignorance. But what about Algy, or whoever came to the lake? If he were not warned it was almost certain that he would try to land, in which case he would be drowned. Yet if he, Biggles, tried to warn him, he would instantly betray himself to the Russians. It was a difficult problem. Really, it came to this: by leaving Algy or Ginger to his fate, he could probably save the papers; conversely, he could save Algy and probably lose the papers. If only he could think of some way of getting the papers into the machine without the machine landing, that would get over the difficulty, but it was not easy to see how this was to be achieved. There appeared to be only one possible way, and not a very hopeful way at that; still, there was no alternative, so he decided to try it. Success would largely depend on the initiative of the pilot. If he perceived what was required of him, then the matter presented no great difficulty – but would he?

Biggles's plan was the employment of the device long used in the Royal Air Force by army cooperation machines for picking up messages from the ground, a system that for years was demonstrated to the public at the R.A.F. display at Hendon. It is comparatively simple. Two thin poles are fixed upright in the ground some twenty feet apart in the manner of goal-posts. Between them a cord is stretched, and to the cord is attached the message. The message in this case would, of course, be the papers. The machine swoops, picks up the line and the message, with a hook which it lowers for the purpose. Here, however, the machine would not be fitted with such a hook, but a clever pilot should have no difficulty in picking up a taut line on his undercarriage wheels. Biggles had no cord, but here again the difficulty was not insuperable. Under his sweater he had a shirt which, torn into strips and joined together, would serve the same purpose, and might even be better than a line since it would be easier to see.

Having reached his decision, Biggles went to work swiftly. First, he found two branches which, stripped of their twigs, would form the posts. There was some difficulty in fixing them in the ground, but he got over this by piling pieces of rock round them. He then took off his shirt and tore it into strips. It was still a bit short, so he made it up to the required length with the lining of his jacket. Having fastened the packet of papers to the centre, he stretched the line across the posts, not tying the ends, but holding them in place with light pieces of wood. Had he fixed the ends, the poles would, of course, be dragged up with the line, and perhaps damage the machine.

All this took some time, and he had barely finished when he heard the machine coming; and presently he made it out, a grey speck in the west, which quickly resolved itself into another Gladiator. The Russians were marching along the far side of the lake and had nearly reached the point nearest to the Blenheim; they had quickened their pace, having realised, apparently, that owing to the water their task was going to be harder than they supposed.

With his signalling pistol in his hand, Biggles dashed down the hill to the bonfire, not caring much now whether the Russians saw him or not, for in any case they would see him when he fired the red light. Strangely enough, they were so intent on their task that they did not once glance in his direction, but went on with what they were doing. Two men, carrying a rope, waded out to the Blenheim, while the rest lined the other end of the rope as if with the intention of dragging the fuselage bodily to the shore. There were cries of alarm, however, when the Gladiator, carrying Finnish markings, suddenly swooped low over the trees and raced across the black water.

Biggles had already lighted his fire, and as there was no wind a column of smoke rose like a pillar into the air, making a signal so conspicuous that the pilot could hardly miss it. He now ran to the edge of the water, clear of the trees, and sent the blazing red flare across the nose of the Gladiator, which swerved to avoid it, and then turned sharply so that the pilot could see whence it came. Biggles saw Ginger's face staring down at him; he just had time to heave a rock into the water and beckon frantically before the machine was compelled to zoom in order to avoid the trees.

Biggles knew that the warning signal had been seen, so he tore back up the hill. He fully expected that he would be shot at, but either the Russians were slow to comprehend what was happening or were too surprised to do anything, and he reached the trees without a shot being fired. When he broke clear of them again on the ridge the Gladiator was circling as if looking for him, and he knew that there was no longer any risk of the machine trying to land. Quite apart from his own signal, the Russians who had waded out to the wreck were now splashing back, and they, too, would have been seen.

From the ridge Biggles first looked down to see what the Russians were doing; as he expected, they were running along the bank in order to reach his side of the lake. Overhead the Gladiator was in a tight turn, whirling round and round, with Ginger staring down from a height of about a hundred feet.

Biggles jabbed his hand frantically at the goal-post arrangement, but Ginger continued to circle, clearly at a loss to know what to do – which in the circumstances was hardly to be wondered at. Biggles groaned as the machine turned away and tore up and down, apparently looking for some place to land – which again was natural enough. Presently it returned, with Ginger waving his arm in a manner that said clearly, 'I can't do anything.'

Biggles snatched up the jacket and waved it. He then ran to the line that supported the papers and shook it;

the shirt being pale blue, he thought it ought to show up fairly well. Conversation was, of course, impossible, so the antics, which to a spectator would have appeared ludicrous, continued. In sheer desperation Biggles spread the jacket wide open on the ground, pointed to it, and then, running to the line, made 'zooming' motions with his hands.

At last Ginger understood. He turned away, banked steeply, and then, cutting his engine, glided at little more than stalling speed towards the line. He missed it, but as he had come to within a few feet of the ground he saw clearly what was required of him and climbed up for another attempt.

Pale with anxiety, Biggles looked at the Russians and saw that they had reached the scene of the avalanche, up which they were scrambling. In ten minutes they would reach him. Shots began to smack against the rocks.

The Gladiator was now coming down again, gliding straight along the ridge, its wings wobbling slightly as they encountered the air currents so near the ground. Again Ginger missed. Worse, one of his wheels struck a post and knocked it over. Biggles, forcing himself to keep calm, put it up again, by which time the Gladiator had circled and was in position for the third attempt. Biggles saw that it must be the last, for the nearest Russians were not more than two hundred yards away. If Ginger failed this time, then he determined to grab the papers, dash down the hill, and throw them on the fire which was still burning. At all events this would prevent them from falling into the hands of the enemy.

This time Ginger did not miss. His wheels went under the line fairly in the middle, and as he zoomed up the line went with him, the ends flapping behind the axle.

Biggles gasped his relief, and then fell into a fever as Ginger began to turn, either to make sure that he had picked up the line or to see what Biggles was doing. Biggles pointed to the west in a peremptory gesture. Ginger waved to show that he understood, and turning again, disappeared over the trees.

Now Biggles had no intention of being taken prisoner if he could avoid it; he took one look at the Russians, now within shouting distance, snatched up his jacket and fled. Yells rose into the air, but he did not stop, nor did he look back. A few shots whistled past him, and then he was under cover of the far side of the ridge, going down it like a mountain goat. He knew that in speed alone lay his only chance of getting away, and he thought he had a fair chance, for he was only lightly clad whereas his pursuers were encumbered with full marching kit – greatcoats, haversacks, rifles, bayonets, and bandoliers. Instinctively he headed for the west, keeping to the trees that hid him from those behind.

It was not easy going, for the ground was rough, scored deeply in places by storm water; there were also fallen trees and outcrops of rock to cope with. Sparing no effort, he raced on, deriving some comfort from the fact that the shouting was growing fainter, from which he judged that he was increasing his lead; but after a while, as his endurance began to give out, he steadied his pace to a jog-trot, and finally to a fast walk. Once he stopped for a moment to listen, but he could hear nothing.

He now began to give some thought to his position. He was a good thirty miles inside the Russian frontier, travelling over much the same route as the unfortunate professor had taken on his dying effort to get the papers to a safe place. Beyond the frontier the country was still wild, so he reckoned that he had not less than fifty miles to go before he could hope to find succour. The only food he had was two biscuits; whether these would be sufficient to keep him going he did not know. He thought they would, for he was in an optimistic mood following the relief of getting rid of the papers. 'It all depends on the weather,' he mused. 'If it holds fine it won't get dark enough to hinder me, so I ought to be able to cover twenty miles before daylight.' Glancing up at the darkening sky, he saw that it was clear of cloud; in fact, if anything, it was a little too clear, for the evening star was gleaming brightly, in a manner that hinted at a return of frosty conditions. There was already a nip in the air. However, he was warm enough while he kept going, and he had no intention of stopping while he was able to go on.

Another comforting thought was this. Assuming that Ginger would get back safely to Oskar, he would lose no time in telling the others what had happened, in which case they might do something about it, although what they would do was not easy to predict, for the ground was much too broken to permit the safe landing of an aircraft. Still, it was reassuring to know that they were aware of his plight. From a high escarpment which he was compelled to climb since it lay across his route, he looked back, but he could see nothing of the Russians, so he strode on, happy in the thought that every minute was taking him nearer home.

An hour passed, and another, but still he kept going, although by now he was beginning to feel the strain. His limbs ached, as did his wounded head, which, in the excitement, he had temporarily forgotten. His rests became more frequent, and he knew that he would soon have to find a haven where he could enjoy a really sustained halt; otherwise he would certainly exhaust himself.

He was now walking through a forest that covered the slope of a fairly steep range of hills. For the most part the soft carpet of pine needles made walking easy, but occasionally a great outcrop of rock would retard his progress, for there was not much light under the trees and he was compelled to pick his way carefully, knowing that a fall must have serious consequences. The country through which he was passing was as savage as the wildest part of Canada, and as uninhabited, and should he break a limb he would certainly die of starvation. He decided that he would explore the next rocks he came to for a cave, or some form of shelter, when he would make a bed of pine needles and have a good rest. There was something disconcerting about the idea of just lying down in the open.

He was not long coming to another mass of rock, and forthwith started to explore the base of it. A dark fissure invited, and he took a pace towards it, only to recoil hurriedly when he was greeted by a low growl. It gave him a nasty turn, for the very last thing in his mind was any thought of wild animals. He had even forgotten that they still existed in Russia.

He was reminded in no uncertain manner. Following the growl, a black mass slowly detached itself from the shadow of the rock and advanced menacingly towards him. It was a bear. It was a large bear, too, and in the dim light it looked even larger than it really was. All the same, it was a formidable beast, and Biggles backed hurriedly. The bear followed. Biggles went faster, whereupon the animal rose on its hind legs and, uttering the most ferocious growls, began to amble after him at a shuffling run.

Biggles bolted. True, he had a pistol in his pocket, but apart from a disinclination to fire a shot which in the still air would be heard for a great distance, and might betray his whereabouts to the Russians, he had more sense than to take on a beast notorious for its vitality with such a weapon at such close range. Finding his way barred by a wall of rock, he went up it with an alacrity that surprised him, to find that the top was more or less level. He looked down. The bear, still growling, made a half-hearted attempt to follow, and then squatted on its haunches, gazing up at him, its forepaws together in an attitude of supplication. Presently it was joined by another, with two cubs. They all sat down, growling softly in their throats, blinking up at the intruder.

'Sorry if I've disturbed the family,' muttered Biggles in a voice heavy with chagrin, for he was angry at being thus held up. He guessed that the thaw had awakened the bears from their winter sleep.

He was answered by more growls.

Biggles shook his head sadly. 'What does one do in a case like this?' he mused. He appeared to be in no immediate danger, but it was obvious that any attempt to leave his perch would be resented by the party underneath; and quite apart from other considerations, the futility of trying to kill outright two full-grown bears with a pistol was only too obvious. He lit a cigarette to think the matter over, hoping that the bears would return to their den and leave him free to go his own way. But evidently the creatures did not like the idea of a stranger being so near their home, for they made no move to depart. The cubs eyed him with frank curiosity, the older ones with hostility.

Biggles considered them moodily. 'Oh, go home,' he told them impatiently.

The bears growled.

Biggles puffed at his cigarette thoughtfully, wondering what madness had induced him to undertake such a crazy quest, a quest that now promised to go on for the duration of the war. A little breeze got up and stirred the pines to uneasy movement. From one of them something that had evidently been lodged on top drifted sluggishly to the ground. It was a strip of pale blue material, frayed at the ends.

Biggles stared at it wide-eyed with consternation. There was no mistaking it. It was a piece of his shirt. Clearly it had broken off his improvised line, but on consideration he felt that this did not necessarily imply that the whole line had come adrift from Ginger's machine. It was quite possible that the end of it had been torn off by the slipstream. After all, he reasoned, Ginger would have flown due west. He himself had run in the same direction, so if a piece of the shirt had come adrift – as it obviously had – it was not remarkable that he should find it. Still, it was an uncomfortable thought that the papers *might* be lying somewhere in the forest. There was nothing he could do about the piece of material, for the bears prevented him from fetching it – not that he was particularly anxious to have it, for there was nothing more it could tell him even if he held it in his hands. So he stayed where he was, stayed while the night wore on interminably to dawn, grey and depressing. The cubs, their interest in the stranger beginning to wane, grew restless, and presently their mother led them off to their lair.

The male parent seemed unable to make up his mind whether to go or to stay. Once or twice he shuffled towards the den, and then, as if loath to lose sight of the intruder, came back, rubbing his paws, and from time to time muttering threats deep in his throat. Finally, however, he made off, and sat just inside the entrance to the cave; Biggles could just see him sitting there, his little piggy eyes sparkling suspiciously. The cave was about forty yards from the rock on which Biggles was perched, and he felt that, provided he did not go near the den, he ought to be able to creep away without upsetting the Bruin family. In any case he would have to try, he decided, otherwise he might sit on the rock indefinitely, which he could not afford to do. So, moving very gently, he slithered to the rear of the rock and dropped quietly to the ground. For a minute he listened, but as he could hear nothing he began to move away. But, quiet as he had been, the bear had heard him, for happening to glance behind, he saw the animal pursuing him at a rolling gait that covered the ground at a surprising speed.

Biggles took to his heels and ran for his life, looking about desperately for a refuge. Trees there were in plenty, but knowing that any tree he could climb the bear would also be able to climb, he left them alone and sped on. For a hundred yards the chase continued, and then ended abruptly. Biggles's foot caught in one of the many roots that projected through the mat of fir needles. He made a desperate effort to save himself, but he was travelling too fast. He stumbled and fell headlong. Even as he fell he whipped the pistol out of his pocket, but in a flash the bear was on him, and with one sweep of a hairy paw knocked the weapon flying. He felt the animal's hot breath beat on his face. Helpless in its ferocious grip, he gave himself up for lost.

CHAPTER XI

Ginger Loses His Temper

Had Biggles, when he had sat upon the rock outside the bear's den, known what had happened to Ginger he would have been more upset than he was. He supposed him to be safe back home, and not for a moment did any other thought occur to him. This was far from the truth.

As a matter of detail, when he arrived over the lake Ginger saw the Russians before he saw Biggles's smoke-signal, for his eyes had gone instinctively to that part of the lake where the wrecked Blenheim lay, and this unexpected factor alone would have prevented him from landing even if it had been possible – unless, of course, he had seen Biggles waiting to be picked up. But this, as we know, was not the case. He saw Biggles's rock splash in the water, and this gave him a pretty shrewd idea of what had happened.

With the events of the next few minutes we are already acquainted, and it may be said that Ginger's relief when he saw the shirt-line on his undercarriage was no less than Biggles's. But his anxiety for Biggles was painful. He felt that he ought to do something, but what could he do? To land was manifestly impossible. It occurred to him to shoot up the Russians with his guns – not that this was likely to help Biggles very much; anyway, Biggles's peremptory signal to him to return home put all other schemes out of his head, and he set about complying with the order. At the back of his mind there was a wild idea of getting a Blenheim and bringing the others over to drop by parachute to Biggles's assistance.

By leaning out of his cockpit he could just see the end strip of shirt; it was flapping wildly in the violent slipstream, and it did not look very safe, for which reason he kept a watchful eye on it as he climbed for height. He had, of course, no means of getting the packet of papers into the cockpit.

He had covered about ten miles of his return journey, and was cruising along at six thousand feet, when to his horror he saw that the end of the line was now so far extended that it reached halfway along the fuselage, trailing back from his right-hand wheel – still far out of reach. This could only mean that the 'drag' on that side of the line was greater than on the other side, in which case it was only a question of time before the whole thing blew off altogether. Here again there was absolutely nothing he could do about it except fly on and hope for the best – that by some miracle the line and its precious burden would hang on at least until he was well inside Finland. But this was not to be. He was actually watching the length of shirt fluttering in the tearing wind when the whole line slipped off and went whirling away behind him.

Immediately a sort of madness came upon him. He felt that the papers were bewitched, possessed of some fantastic influence which made their recovery impossible. He began to hate the sight of them. He had already turned, and staring ahead, he saw the length of rag, sagging under the weight in the middle, sinking slowly earthward. Thrusting the joystick forward savagely, he went at it like a bull at a gate, knowing that he would have no difficulty in overtaking it before it reached the ground; but just what was going to happen when he did reach it he could not think. He had never attempted anything of the sort before; not in his wildest imaginings had he visualised a chase so utterly ridiculous.

The frayed strip of rag seemed to float towards him. At first he aimed his nose straight towards the middle of it, but then, terrified lest the flashing airscrew should hit the papers and cut them to shreds, he gave the joystick an extra push, and at the same time thrust an arm into the air, hoping the strip would catch on it; but this was expecting too much. He ducked instinctively as the crazy line, strung out across the sky, flashed over his head. It missed his hand by about a foot. Looking back to see what had happened to it, to his unspeakable joy he saw that it had caught across the fin, and was now streaming back on either side of his tail. Gulping with emotion, he steadied his pace and began to climb steadily back to his original altitude, all the time watching the streamer. He felt that the whole thing was becoming preposterous – ludicrous. 'I'm going crazy,' he told himself.

Indeed, the recovery of the elusive papers had assumed a similarity to one of those frightful nightmares when one goes on and on trying to do something, but all the time getting farther and farther away from success. It is hardly a matter for wonder that he began to ask himself if the absurd situation was really taking place or whether he was dreaming. If, at this juncture, he had encountered an enemy fighter, things would certainly have gone badly with him, for he did not even glance at the sky. Every nerve, every fibre of his body was concentrated on the papers.

He covered about five miles and then, for no apparent reason, the rags slipped off again, and went spinning away to the rear. He nearly screamed with rage, and as he tore after them he grated his teeth with fury. Never had he hated anything so wholeheartedly as he hated those papers, for which reason his antics, to a watcher, must have raised serious doubts as to his sanity.

In his first charge Ginger missed the papers altogether. In the second he caught the line with a wing-tip, causing the other end to whip round so that the packet actually hit him on the head before bouncing clear again into space. A sound that was something between a groan and a howl of mortification broke from his lips. 'I'm balmy!' he told himself pathetically. 'Balmy! The thing's got me down.'

His final effort was the most hair-raising, for by this time he was perilously near the ground and it was now or never; furthermore, his nose was tilted down at an alarming angle. The rag caught on one of the blades of his propeller, spun round for a moment like a crazy windmill, and then flew to pieces. The packet, detached, described a graceful arc, and then, bursting like a star-shell, shed the papers over the landscape; they floated slowly earthwards, like seagulls landing on smooth water.

Ginger dragged the joystick back just in time. His wheels brushed the tree-tops as he levelled out and then shot upward in a terrified zoom. Perspiration broke out on his forehead, and his expression was that of a man whom – as the Romans used to say – the gods had deprived of his wits. At that moment his rage was such that had he had the papers in his hand he would have torn them to shreds with his teeth. He loathed them and everything to do with them.

Swallowing hard, he cut his engine and began to glide back towards the place where the papers had fallen, forcing himself to some semblance of normality. He knew that somehow he had got to recover the documents – but how? He could see them clearly, little white spots on the ground near a group of pines that stood alone at the end of a valley.

He began to fly round looking for a place to land. Actually, there was nowhere where a pilot in his right mind would have attempted to land, but in his present mood Ginger was not particular. Desperate, he was ready to take almost any chance – which, in fact, is what he did. Farther down the valley there was a brook. Beside it a strip of comparatively level ground offered possibilities. It was so narrow that a landing could be attempted in only one direction, but as there was no wind this really did not matter. He doubted if the strip were long enough for him to get down and run to a standstill without colliding with something, for there were more trees at the far end; but he could at any rate try. Cutting his engine again, he began to go down, side-slipping first one way and then the other in order to lose height without an excess of forward speed.

'If I get down without busting something I shall be the world's greatest pilot,' he told himself grimly.

Judging by results he was not the world's greatest pilot, although his effort was a creditable one. The wheels touched, and the winter-browned grass, which turned out to be longer than he had thought, at once began to pull him up. For a moment a genuine hope surged through him that he had achieved the apparently impossible; but alas for his hopes! Hidden in the sere, tussocky grass were small outcrops of rock, and he saw them too late. He missed several by inches, and again he hoped that luck might favour him and all would be well. Slower and slower ran the Gladiator; and then, just at the last moment, his wheel struck a rock. There was a terrific bang as the tyre burst; the machine swerved wildly and then stopped.

With the slow deliberation of a martyr going to execution, Ginger got down, walked round the wing and looked at the wheel. The tyre had been torn clean off and the rim was buckled. That was the only damage the machine had suffered, but it was enough. He might as well have smashed the whole machine to pieces for all the chance he had of getting it off the ground again.

'Well, that's that,' he told himself in a curiously calm voice, for now that the worst had happened there was no need to worry about it.

In a mechanical sort of way he collected a rifle from the bottom of his cockpit, a weapon which he had brought against emergency; then, leaving the machine where it stood, he walked up the valley to recover the papers. He had no difficulty in finding them, for they lay close together, so he collected all he could see and folded them in a bundle, which he wrapped in the original piece of canvas. He was putting it in his pocket when a horrid thought struck him – the same thought that had occurred to Biggles the previous day. Up to this moment he had assumed that all he had to do now was walk home, but he realised suddenly that this would take some time; in the meanwhile, when he did not return, Algy would take off and fly to the lake, in which case, if he did not drown himself trying to land on the water, he would probably fall into the hands of the Russians.

Ginger sat down abruptly, sick with apprehension. He had not forgotten Biggles, but he could not see how he could help him, although if (as he hoped) he had escaped from the Russians, he should now be on his way home; indeed, he might be only a few miles away.

This put an entirely new idea into Ginger's head. If, in fact, Biggles was travelling westward, and he, Ginger, set off eastward, or even waited where he was, they ought soon to make contact, when they could go home together. Then yet another thought occurred to him. Somewhere near the lake must be Biggles's Gladiator. Assuming that it was intact, it ought to be possible to get one of the wheels and put it on his own machine, which would then be in a condition to fly home.

With all these conjectures racing through his mind, he found it hard to make a decision. The point he had to decide was this: should he push on alone and try to reach Finland, or would it be wiser to walk back over his track in the hope of meeting Biggles? In the end he decided on a compromise. He would walk back a few miles, find a high spot that commanded a view of the country, and there wait for Biggles. If when morning came Biggles was not in sight, he would make for the frontier. He did not overlook the possibility of colliding with a party of Russians, which made him disinclined to keep the papers on his person, so his first action was to find a hiding-place for them. If he failed to locate Biggles he would pick them up again on his way back. The group of trees at the end of the valley offered possibilities, and after hunting round for a little while he found a hole under the root of one of the trees; in it he placed the packet, and sealed the mouth of the hole with a large stone. This done, he set off towards the east, making his way up the side of a hill, from the top of which he hoped to get a good view of the country beyond.

Darkness, or comparative darkness, fell before he reached the top, so that he found his view somewhat restricted, but as far as he could make out he was surrounded by rugged, untamed country. A feeling of loneliness assailed him; it was, moreover, cold on the desolate hill-top; so, still heading eastward, he made his way thoughtfully down to the forest that clothed its flank. It was warmer under the trees, but darker, dark enough to make travel both tedious and dangerous, so he found a fairly snug corner under an overhanging rock and settled down to pass the night as well as he could.

For a long time he lay awake, not trying to sleep, but after a while nature triumphed and he passed from restless dozing to real sleep. And during his sleep he had an extraordinary dream – extraordinary both on account of its nature and vividness. He dreamed that Biggles called to him from some way off, telling him to go home. He remembered the words distinctly, for so real, so ringing had been the voice that it was hard to believe that it had occurred only in a dream. Biggles had cried out, 'Oh, go home.'

Not a little disturbed by this strange, not to say startling, occurrence, Ginger sat up and saw that the grey light of dawn was penetrating the tree-tops, flooding the forest with a wan, weird light. He felt refreshed after his rest and better able to tackle the situation, so he picked up the rifle and was about to move off when he heard a sound he little expected to hear in such a lonely place. It sounded like a man running – not only running, but running for his life. The swift patter of feet flying over the fir needles came swiftly towards him, and he crouched back against the rock trusting that he would not be seen, holding the rifle at the ready should it be required.

Suddenly the runner burst into sight round a buttress of rock, so close that he could have touched him. It was Biggles. Looking neither to left nor right, he tore on.

Ginger was so astounded, so shaken, that he could only stare, his jaw sagging foolishly. He barely had time to wonder what Biggles was running away from when it appeared – a fur-clad fury in the form of a bear. Hardly knowing what he was doing, he raced after the brute, hesitating to shout in case he called the bear's attention to himself. And so for a moment or two the curious procession tore on through the trees, the bear chasing Biggles and Ginger chasing the bear, with perhaps a score of paces between them. Then, to Ginger's horror, Biggles stumbled and sprawled headlong. In a flash the bear was on him.

It is doubtful if Ginger could have stopped even had he wanted to. The impetus of his spurt carried him right up to the animal. Without hesitation he clapped the muzzle of the rifle to its ear and pulled the trigger. The report shattered the silence. The bear, with a grunt, collapsed, and then, toppling over sideways, went rolling down the hill, down and down, until it was finally brought to a stop by the trunk of a tree.

Ginger never forgot the expression on Biggles's face as he sat up. He was as white as a sheet. Utter incredulity struggled with profound relief.

'What in the name of all that's crazy are *you* doing here?' he gasped.

CHAPTER XII

Another Blow

Before Ginger could reply there came growls, fast approaching, from the direction of the rocks.

'Here, come on, let's get out of this,' muttered Biggles, and dashed off through the trees followed by Ginger.

Not until they had put some distance between them and the bear-infested rocks did Biggles pull up. He found a log and sat on it. His first question, asked in ones of biting sarcasm, was, 'Where are those thrice bedevilled papers?'

'They fell off. I tried to land to pick them up, and bust a wheel,' answered Ginger mournfully.

Biggles buried his face in his hands and groaned.

Ginger described in detail what had happened while Biggles listened in mute resignation.

'You know, kid,' murmured Biggles in a strained voice when Ginger had finished, 'this business is getting me dizzy. It's uncanny, it's crazy, it's one of those stories that goes on and on always coming back to the same place. Writers have made a big song about Jason and the Golden Fleece. Pah! Jason did nothing. He ought to have had a crack at this job. I don't often give way to despair, but by the anti-clockwise propeller of my sainted aunt, I'm getting to the state when I could throw myself down and burst into tears – like a little girl who's lost her bag of sweets. Well, I suppose it's no use sitting here. Let's go and look for the papers – we shall probably find they've been eaten by a rabbit.'

'What do we do in that case – catch the rabbit?' grinned Ginger.

'Let's wait till we get there, then I'll tell you. Only one thing I ask you if you have any respect for my sanity. Don't, when we get there, tell me that you've forgotten which tree they're under. It only needs one more little thing to give me shrieking hysterics.'

'Oh, I reckon I can find the place all right,' returned Ginger moodily.

'By the way, why were you coming this way?' asked Biggles. 'Why didn't you make for home?'

'I aimed to find your Gladiator, get a wheel off it, put it on my own kite and fly back.'

Biggles started. 'Say, that's an idea! We might do that. In fact, I think we shall have to go to the lake anyway, because Algy will be over this afternoon, and we ought to let him know that we're all right.'

'The Russians may still be there.'

'We shall have to risk that. You know Algy; if we're not there to send him home he's likely to go on to Moscow. Well, we'd better make a start. I reckon it's a good twelve miles to the lake. If we keep going we ought to get there before Algy; then all we have to do is take a wheel off the Gladiator, come back and pick up the papers, put the wheel on your machine, and fly home – I hope.'

They set off, Ginger carrying the rifle, and after making a detour round the bear-den, bore due east. Both were beginning to feel the need for food, but they said nothing about it, knowing that none was available. They plodded on steadily, stopping only to reconnoitre the country from the tops of the hills that lay in their path. However, they saw no movement of any sort, and shortly after midday they reached the western edge of the lake.

They now proceeded with greater caution, moving quietly from tree to tree, often stopping to listen and scouting the ground thoroughly as they advanced. However, everything was silent, from which they judged that the Russians had departed; otherwise so large a number of men would, they felt, have given some sign of their presence. At last they reached a point from where they could see the fuselage of the Blenheim, now hauled up on the bank, apparently as the Russians had left it.

'Let's go across and have a forage round,' suggested Ginger.

'I doubt if we shall find any food; I expect the Russians will have stripped the machine of everything portable,' answered Biggles. 'However, we may as well go round that way.'

Still keeping sharp watch, they advanced, not a little relieved to find the lake deserted, for it simplified what, had the Russians been there, would have been a difficult task. At last they reached the Blenheim, only to find, as Biggles had predicted, that it had been stripped of everything of value. Even the instruments had been taken.

'Well, it was only to be expected,' observed Biggles. 'After all, the salvage was too valuable to be left lying here.'

There were some odd scraps of food, chiefly pieces of broken biscuit, lying on an empty case in the cabin, where the Russians had obviously made at least one meal out of the provisions the Blenheim had carried. These odd scraps the airmen ate with satisfaction.

'There seems nothing more to stay here for,' remarked Biggles when the last scrap had been consumed. 'Let's go across to the Gladiator. We'll get a wheel off, and then gather some twigs to light a fire as soon as Algy shows up.' They set off again, following the bank.

Now up to this point Biggles had not been concerned at not seeing the Gladiator, although he had several times looked in its direction, because he had forced it as far as possible under the trees. But as they drew nearer and he still could not see it, although he knew exactly where he had left it, a puzzled expression dawned on his face.

'That's a funny thing. We ought to be able to see it from here,' he said once as they hurried on.

'Just where did you leave it?'

'Under the trees – near the foot of the avalanche.'

'Perhaps it's behind that tangle of rubbish.'

'If it is then I didn't put it there,' declared Biggles.

'Maybe the Russians found it.'

'I don't think there's any doubt about that; they'd see it when they were chasing round after me, at the time when you were trying to pick up my shirt. But it didn't occur to me that, since they were unable to fly it off, they would do anything with it.'

'It was a valuable machine, and intact,' Ginger pointed out.

'Wes, I agree, but even so—'

When they reached the spot the matter was settled beyond all doubt or question. The Gladiator had gone; apparently it had been removed in sections, for round the place where it had stood the ground was trampled into mud by those who had done the work.

Ginger looked at Biggles. Biggles looked at Ginger. He smiled. 'We certainly ought to have looked at our horoscopes before we started on this jaunt,' he observed. 'Did you ever know things go so awkwardly? I must say the Russians were pretty smart shifting all this stuff; they can't have been gone very long.'

'Let's have a look.'

They scrambled up the ridge above the avalanche – the same ridge from where, so short a while before, they had looked down on the frozen lake at the end of their sledge-ride.

'There they go,' said Biggles, pointing, but taking care to keep below the skyline.

In the distance a large body of men, with several vehicles, was moving eastwards across an open plain. The vehicles were piled high, and even the men were heavily loaded.

'Yes, there they go – and there goes the Gladiator,' said Ginger bitterly.

'There is this about it,' resumed Biggles. 'They have at least left us in possession of the lake. I only hope von Stalhein has given up the search for the papers and gone back to Germany. I should feel easier with him out of the way.'

'Hm. I wonder what happened to him? It isn't like him to give up so easily.'

'He isn't here, anyway, and that's all that matters at the moment,' asserted Biggles. 'We'll stick around until Algy comes; we'll give him the O.K. and then make for home. Let's get a bit of a fire together and then sit down and rest while we have the chance. We've got a long walk in front of us.'

So they sat down and discussed the situation until they heard the sound for which they were waiting – the roar of an aeroplane coming from the west.

Biggles stared for a moment at the approaching aircraft. 'It's Algy,' he confirmed. 'At least, it's a Gladiator, and

I don't know who else it could be. Let's light the fire.'
Suiting the action to the words, he put a match to the
little heap of twigs, which soon sent a coil of smoke
curling upwards. This done, they stood on the ridge in
as conspicuous a position as they could find.

Algy, in the Gladiator, was not long spotting them; the
machine, after roaring low over the smoke, glided back
with the pilot waving.

Biggles raised his arms with his 'thumbs up' (a signal
that is universally understood to mean that all is well), and
then pointed to the west. To emphasise this last point, that
they were starting for home, he began to walk quickly in
that direction.

But Algy did not go. He merely circled round, in much
the same state of mind that Ginger had been in on the
previous day. After a while he climbed higher, flew straight
for a minute or two, and then glided back, very low. As he
passed over the two white faces staring up at him his arm
appeared over the side of the cockpit and a small object
dropped like a stone.

Biggles ran and picked it up. It was Algy's cigarette case.
Inside was a message written on a page torn from a pilot's
notebook. He read it aloud.

'Understand you have both crashed. Am returning
home to fetch food; light fire when I come back so I can
see you. I will drop grub. If you reach possible landing
field, wait, and make signal. I'll come down. If this is O.K.
raise both arms in the air.'

Biggles looked up. The machine was still circling. He
held up his arms. Instantly the machine dipped its wings
to show that the signal was understood and then bore away
to the west.

Biggles and Ginger watched it go. 'Well, that's something achieved anyway,' declared Biggles. 'He does at least know how we're fixed; and knowing the line we shall take, he ought to be able to keep in touch with us. If he can keep us going with food we shall take no harm – in fact, getting home ought to be a fairly easy matter. Say, what's that?' He spun round in alarm as the noise of the Gladiator's engine seemed suddenly to become intensified. Then his face grew pale. 'Look!' he gasped, pointing.

Ginger was already looking, and had seen what Biggles had seen. Three Messerschmitts were dropping out of the sky like bullets on to the tail of the cruising Gladiator.

'Good heavens! He hasn't even seen them,' said Biggles in a strangled voice.

Ginger said nothing. He could only stare.

But if Algy hadn't seen the Messerschmitts when Biggles had spoken, he very soon did so, as the behaviour of his machine proved. He was too old a war pilot to be caught napping. As the German machines came within range, the Gladiator swept up in a tight half roll, turned as it came out, and sent a stream of bullets at its nearest aggressor.

The three Messerschmitts broke formation instantly and the leader went into a glide as if his engine had been hit. He did not return to the combat. But the two that remained attacked the Gladiator with skill and ferocity, keeping one on each side, but as the lone machine gave neither of them a sitting shot the battle remained indecisive. In his heart Biggles knew that such an unequal combat could not continue long, for neither in performance nor armament is the Gladiator, which is now an old type, a match for the Messerschmitt. Further, Algy had to press on towards home, or try to, for his petrol supply was limited; but every time he tried to break away the Messerschmitts, being faster, were on him, and he had to resort to aerobatics to keep out of their fire, which he returned as often as occasion offered. Then, suddenly, the Gladiator seemed to draw away.

'They've had enough!' cried Ginger jubilantly. 'Good old Algy!'

Biggles shook his head. 'Forget it,' he said bitterly. 'They're keeping away from his fire, that's all. They'll keep out of range and get him by using their cannon. Algy won't be able to get close enough to do them any harm.'

The truth of this assumption was soon all too apparent. The Messerschmitts, keeping out of range of the Gladiator's machine-guns, opened fire with their cannon. As soon as Algy realised this he took the only possible course open to him – he put his machine in a turn and held it there, to prevent the Messerschmitts from getting their sights on him. Yet whenever opportunity offered he darted in and attacked. This was all right up to a point, but Algy's trouble was his limited fuel supply, which made it imperative that he should cross the frontier before it gave out. Twice he made a dash for home, but each time he was compelled to turn and face his opponents as they closed in on him.

The end of such a fight was inevitable. Several times shells appeared to burst right against the Gladiator, causing those on the ground to hold their breath in anguished suspense. All three machines had now drawn away to the west for a distance of two or three miles, so that it was not easy to follow the battle. Several times the machines appeared to pass very close to each other, and after one such encounter the Gladiator was seen to falter; then its nose went down and it dived in a straight line for the treetops. More than that Biggles and Ginger could not see, for rising ground and intervening trees obstructed the view. The two Messerschmitts circled for a minute or two over the place where the Gladiator had disappeared, and then made off to the south-east.

'He's down,' said Ginger in a dull voice.

'It was bound to end that way,' muttered Biggles harshly. He was as white as a sheet. 'Come on, let's find him,' he added, and broke into a run.

Panting, scrambling over obstacles that lay in their path, often stumbling and sometimes falling, they ran on, still hoping against hope that by some miracle Algy had escaped death, but in any case anxious to know the worst. Twilight closed in as they ran on.

'The crash must be somewhere about here,' declared Biggles at last, slowing down. 'It was over these trees that he went down.'

'Thank God the machine didn't take fire, anyway,' whispered Ginger fervently through dry lips. 'If it had we should have seen the glow. I—' He broke off and turned a startled face to Biggles as a shrill whistle pierced the trees. 'Why, that must be him!' he cried joyfully.

Biggles's face lighted up. 'He's got away with it after all,' he shouted excitedly. 'Hi! Algy! Where are you?'

'This way.'

They dashed in the direction of the voice, and presently they saw Algy coming towards them. He seemed a bit unsteady on his feet, and he was mopping blood from his chin, but he was grinning broadly.

'What have *you* got to laugh about?' demanded Biggles. 'You gave us the fright of our lives.'

'The bloke who can walk away from a crash has always got plenty to laugh about,' declared Algy.

'Are you hurt?'

'Nothing to speak of.'

'Well, you obviously haven't any bones broken, and that's the main thing,' said Biggles thankfully. 'What happened?'

'They got my engine, so I pancaked on the treetops, which, as you will notice, are pretty thick hereabouts. I've made harder landings on open ground.'

'Where's the crash?'

'Just over here.' Algy led the way to the spot where the Gladiator, its fabric badly torn, still hung balanced precariously on the pliable tops of the fir trees. Drops of oil, or petrol, or both, dripped steadily from the machine and splashed on the carpet of fir needles.

'I think I did myself most damage getting down the tree,' remarked Algy. 'That's how I damaged my chin – stubbed it on a dead branch.'

Biggles regarded the aircraft sympathetically. 'Well, she'll never fly again,' he announced.

'No, but she might help another machine to fly,' cried Ginger hopefully.

Biggles started. 'By jingo! You're right there,' he agreed enthusiastically. 'That's an idea. We'll shake her down and borrow one of her wheels.'

Algy stared in amazement. 'What's all this?' he demanded. 'What the dickens do you want a wheel for? Are you thinking of playing hoops on the way home?'

Biggles laughed, and briefly explained the situation.

'But surely you've got the papers?' burst out Algy.

'No. We had them and lost them again,' confessed Biggles. 'That is to say, I had them and passed them on

125

to Ginger, and he's hidden them. He's tucked them into a hole under a tree somewhere.'

Algy screwed up his face in an expression of agony and leaned weakly against a tree. 'Suffering alligators!' he lamented. 'And after all this you *still* haven't got those blithering documents. I thought you'd got them in your pocket. I shall go off my rocker if this goes on much longer, and spend the rest of my days crawling about looking for scraps of paper.'

'I reckon we all shall,' agreed Biggles. 'However, Ginger knows where they are, and as far as we know there's nothing to stop us getting them, so that's something to be thankful for. Let's get this machine to the ground for a start, and pull one of her wheels off.'

Getting the machine to the ground, however, was by no means easy, and in the end Ginger had to climb up a tree and shake. 'Hush-a-bye baby on the tree top,' he crooned, as he swayed to and fro, allowing the machine to sink slowly through the branches.

'Don't play the fool,' cried Biggles. 'We don't want to have to carry you home – we've plenty on our hands without that. Look out, she's coming.'

With a rending of branches and a tearing of fabric, the machine crashed to the ground. After that it did not take long to knock out the pin and remove a wheel.

'That's grand,' declared Ginger. 'It was most thoughtful of you to drop in like this, Algy, old pal; otherwise we should have had to pad the hoof all the way home.'

Biggles picked up the wheel. 'You know where the papers are, so lead on,' he told Ginger. 'I shall feel happier when they're in my pocket.'

'How long have we been on this job?' inquired Algy as they set off through the trees.

'Oh, about four days,' returned Biggles.

'That's what I made it, but it seems more like four months.'

'Don't worry, we're on the road home now,' said Biggles reassuringly.

'I suppose you haven't overlooked the possibility of the two Messerschmitt pilots going home and reporting a crash hereabouts, in which case somebody might come over to look for it?'

'No, I haven't lost sight of that possibility,' answered Biggles, 'but I don't think we need worry about that. Even if somebody did come, by the time he reached here we should be miles away. He's welcome to what's left of the Gladiator.'

'We ought to have set fire to it,' said Ginger.

'I did think of it, but it seemed crazy to light a beacon which would have been seen for miles, and bring anybody who happened to be about straight to the spot.'

'You're dead right,' agreed Algy. 'The thing is to get home.'

As they topped the last rise that overlooked the valley wherein Ginger's Gladiator stood, and at the near end of which was the clump of trees where he had concealed the papers, Ginger started back with a cry of consternation. He looked at the others with an expression of agitation. 'Keep back,' he said tersely.

'What is it?' asked Biggles quickly, sensing that something was wrong.

'Take a look, but be careful not to show yourself,' replied Ginger in a voice that was tremulous in spite of his efforts to keep it calm.

The others knelt and peered over the ridge into the valley below. Dotted with tents and fires, around which numbers of men were moving or resting, the valley was now a camp. What the Russians were doing there, or why they had come there, none of them could at first imagine, but they were there, and that was all that really mattered.

Biggles sat down on a rock and threw the wheel aside. 'To think that I've carried this blessed thing all this way for nothing!' he exclaimed disgustedly.

'Yes, that certainly has torn it,' muttered Algy.

Biggles looked at Ginger. 'Couldn't you think of any other place to hide those papers than in the middle of a Russian camp?' he said with bitter sarcasm.

'And couldn't the Russians, with the whole blessed country to choose from, find a place to camp without choosing the spot where I hid the papers?' answered Ginger bitingly.

'Where did you leave the machine?'

'Up the far end of the valley.'

'That means that the Russians will have found it, so what they'll leave behind when they go – if they go – won't be worth picking up. There even seems to be a tent among the trees where you say you hid the papers. Somebody will only have to find them and take them away to finish a really good job of work. I suppose there was no possibility of anybody finding the papers, was there?'

Ginger looked dubious. 'Well, I couldn't do more than I did. I shoved them in a hole and put a stone on it. Anyway, I thought no one ever came here. I wasn't to know that a blinking army was going to take up residence on the spot. What are we going to do about it?'

'I suggest that we all go and jump into the nearest lake and put ourselves out of our misery,' suggested Algy gloomily. 'If anyone ever mentions papers to me again I'll—'

'Yes, I know,' interrupted Biggles. 'We all feel that way. Let's rest for a minute or two and get hold of ourselves. Maybe I can think of something.'

Biggles cupped his chin in his hands and gazed unseeingly across the dreary landscape that they had just traversed.

CHAPTER XIII

Von Stalhein Again

For some little while Biggles sat still, deep in thought, while the night slowly grew darker; but at last he drew a deep breath.

'Well,' he said evenly, 'we may as well face the facts. Let's get them in order. To start with, we can wash out all idea of flying home in Ginger's Gladiator. The camp extends right down the valley, so it would be foolish to suppose that it hasn't been discovered. Even if it were just as Ginger left it, we couldn't hope to get a wheel off it without being discovered, and even if we did we couldn't get it off the ground because the tents are in the way. That means we've got to walk home. Point number two is, we must try to get the papers. It's dark enough to prevent our uniforms being recognised, so it shouldn't be impossible to get to the tree, recover the papers, and get away without being spotted. It depends largely on what's happening in the trees. There's a tent pitched there, and as it stands apart from the others we may presume that it belongs to the commanding officer. If that is so, we shall have to keep an eye open for messengers and orderlies. Another point which should not be overlooked is this. I may be wrong, but I don't think these troops are concerned with us. It looks more like a concentration getting ready to attack the Finns in a new theatre of war. The Finns ought to know about it, and it's up to us to get the information to them. After all, until we started this scatterbrain business of chasing a bunch of papers our job was reconnaissance, to spot just such troop movements as this.' Biggles paused for a moment.

'This is my scheme,' he continued. 'I'm going down to get the papers, and since delay won't make the job any easier I'm going right now. Ginger will have to come with me to show me where they are, otherwise I might be groping round on my hands and knees for an hour or more. Algy, you'll stay here. If by any chance we fail to come back, abandon us and the papers; make your way back home as fast as you can, tell the Finns about these troops, and explain to Raymond what's happened. If after that you feel like snooping back here in the hope of finding out what has become of us, do so, but if you take my tip you'll keep the right side of the frontier. That's all. Are you ready Ginger?'

'Ay, ay, sir.'

Biggles took out his pistol, which he had recovered after the bear incident, and examined the mechanism to make sure that it was working properly. 'Leave your rifle here with Algy,' he told Ginger. 'It'll be in the way. In any case, he's more likely to need it than you are. Let's go.'

There was no great danger in approaching the camp, for although it was not absolutely dark, visibility was reduced to a short distance, and it was unlikely that they would be seen. Even if they were, it appeared probable that they would be mistaken for Russians, for a number of troops were wandering about outside the camp, apparently fetching wood for the fires.

With the coppice between them and the main camp, they went slowly down the hill, keeping sharp watch for sentries. However, they saw none, and presently stood within a score of paces of the group of pines wherein Ginger had hidden the papers. It was now possible to see more clearly what was happening inside the coppice. A tent had been erected, and yellow light penetrating through the fabric proved fairly conclusively that it was occupied. Close to the tent a fire smouldered between two pieces of stone on which stood a soup-kettle.

'Now, which is the tree?' said Biggles quietly.

Ginger grimaced. 'Well, it's a bit difficult to explain,' he whispered. 'There are so many trees so much alike that whatever I said might refer to any one of them. Once in the trees I could go straight to the spot. You'd better let me go – or let me come with you.'

The wisdom of this was so apparent that Biggles did not dispute it. He looked round cautiously to make sure that nobody was near. 'Come on,' he said softly.

Taking advantage of every scrap of cover, they made their way into the trees. Nobody saw them – or if they did they took no notice. Yet within hailing distance were several hundred enemy troops; the babble of their voices drowned all other sound. Biggles smiled grimly at this example of slack discipline, but he was not surprised, for he had heard something of Russian military methods from the Finns. On the face of it, the recovery of the papers appeared now to be only a matter of seconds.

Ginger went straight to the tree under which he had hidden them, then stopped abruptly with a quick intake of breath.

'What's wrong?' asked Biggles tersely.

'The stone I put over the hole has been moved.'

'Are you sure?'

'Certain. It was a big one. I should see it if it were here.'

'But who would move it, and for what? Are you positive this is the tree?'

Ginger pointed to the stones that flanked the cooking fire. 'It was one of those,' he said.

'Never mind, get the papers.'

Ginger dropped on his knees and thrust a hand into the hole. He turned a distraught face upwards. 'They've gone!'

'Impossible!'

'But I tell you they have.'

'You must be mistaken in the tree.'

'No. This was the one. The hole is here to prove it.'

'How far inside the hole did you put the papers?'

'Only just inside. I was afraid to push them too far in in case they slipped farther – too far for me to get my hand in.'

Biggles clicked his tongue. 'The fellow who moved the stone must have seen them and taken them out. He probably lit the fire with them, not realising their importance. Few of these Russians can read.'

Ginger stood up and brushed the dirt off his hands. 'Well, that settles that,' he said. 'Unless you're going to walk into the camp looking for the cook, we might as well go home.'

Biggles stood still, staring down at the empty hole. And as he stood there a laugh burst from the tent. It seemed so close and so unexpected that he spun round, gun raised. Then he turned a startled face to Ginger. 'You heard that?'

'Yes.'

'Did it – remind you – of anyone?' Biggles's voice was hard.

'Yes.'

'Who?'

'Von Stalhein.'

'You're right. He's in that tent. But he doesn't often laugh. What's he got to laugh at?'

'I should say he's got the papers.'

Biggles nodded. 'That's about it. He's here with the Russian Commander. The cook found the papers and had the wit to take them to the tent. Von Stalhein would recognise them at once. No wonder he's laughing. That's twice he's tumbled on them by accident. He certainly has had all the luck this time. Have you got a knife on you?'

'Yes.' Ginger took it out – a small pen-knife – opened it and passed it to Biggles.

Biggles crept up to the back of the tent.

Ginger crouched back against a tree just behind him. 'Look out!' he hissed.

Biggles dropped flat. He was just in time. A Russian soldier appeared out of the gloom carrying a long butcher's knife in his hand; he went straight to the fire, thrust something into the pot and then sat down, presumably to wait for the stuff, whatever it was, to cook.

Biggles rose to his feet like a shadow and crept up behind the Russian. He was in no state to wait there for perhaps an hour until the dish was ready. At the last moment he trod on a twig. It snapped. The Russian turned sharply, saw Biggles, and with a startled exclamation half rose to his feet. But Biggles moved like a flash. His arm swung down. There was a thud as the butt of his pistol struck the Russian's head. With a grunt the man fell across his own fire. Biggles dragged him clear and returned to Ginger.

'I hate doing that sort of thing, it's so primitive,' he said disgustedly, 'but there was nothing else for it. We couldn't squat here for an hour or more while he was making a stew – or whatever he was doing. Stand fast.'

With the pen-knife now in his right hand Biggles went again to the tent. Very slowly he forced the point through the fabric, and then withdrew it. He put his eye to the slit. For a moment he stood motionless, then he returned again to Ginger.

'Von Stalhein is there with a Russian – he looks like a general. They've got a table between them and the papers are on it. Stay here.'

'What are you going to do?'

'Get the papers – what else? You look after things outside.'

Before Ginger could express the alarm he felt at this drastic step, Biggles had gone, and there was no longer anything furtive about his manner. He went straight to the flap that covered the entrance, threw it aside, and went in, his pistol held just in front of his right hip.

The two men looked up sharply at the intrusion. They half moved forward, but the tone of Biggles's voice halted them – or perhaps it was the expression on his face.

It was one of the few occasions when Biggles saw the German look really surprised. 'Keep still,' he rasped. To von Stalhein in particular he added, 'Tell your pal that one squeak from either of you will be the signal for me to start shooting – and keep your hands in sight. I'm in no mood for monkey business and you'd be wise to believe that.'

Grim-faced, his eyes as hard as ice, his lips pressed in a straight line, Biggles stepped forward, collected the papers with his left hand into a heap, and rolled them into a wad. 'I'll take care of these,' he said. Then he called Ginger.

Ginger appeared in the tent doorway looking some-what shaken.

Biggles thrust the papers at him. 'Take these,' he said. 'Get going.'

Without a word Ginger put the papers in his pocket, turned about and disappeared.

'Now listen, von Stalhein,' said Biggles quietly, 'and listen carefully. A little while ago you accused me of outplaying my luck. You've had more than your share of luck in this party, but don't overdo it. I'm going outside now. You'll stay here. Try leaving this tent and you're apt to meet a slug coming the other way.' Biggles backed out.

The moment he was outside he went quickly round the tent loosening all the guy ropes except two; he then went to the fallen Russian, snatched up his knife, and slashed at the remaining cords. There was a startled cry from within, but before the occupants could get out the tent collapsed. Two jerking humps showed where von Stalhein and his companion were struggling to free themselves from the heavy canvas.

Biggles waited for no more. Turning, he dashed through the trees and raced up the hill to where he had left Algy. He found Ginger waiting; they were both in a state of agitation and uttered exclamations of relief when he appeared.

'Come on,' snapped Biggles, 'jump to it. We've got to get all the start we can before von Stalhein gets his mob on our heels, and that won't take very long. I'm going to make a dash for the frontier.' With that he set off at a steady run towards the west. There was no road, no path, not even a track, so all he could do was to set a course in a westerly direction.

'Here, you'd better have these papers,' said Ginger.

Biggles took them and put them in his pocket.

It was not long before a clamour in the camp told them that von Stalhein was mustering all his forces for the pursuit, but this was only to be expected and it left Biggles unperturbed. Endurance would now decide who reached the frontier first, and in this respect he felt that, in spite of all their handicaps, they ought to be able to hold their own with the Russians. None of them wasted breath in conversation; with their elbows against their sides they ran on, up hill and down dale, through woods, splashing through swamps formed by the melting snow, round unclimbable masses of rock, and sometimes making detours to avoid lakes. Later they struck a lake that lay right across their path, forcing them to turn to the north seeking a way round it. That there was a way Biggles knew, for he had marked the lake from the air.

They were still running, following the bank, when, unexpectedly, they came to a lonely farmhouse, or the house of a charcoal burner – they didn't stop to inquire which. A dog rushed out at them, barking furiously. Biggles snatched up a clod and hurled it at the animal, whereupon it retired, growling furiously.

'This way!' he cried, for he had spotted something that pleased him more than a little. It was a boat, a rough, homemade dug-out moored to a tree-stump. A man was shouting, but he took no notice. 'In you get,' he told the others, and they tumbled into the primitive craft. Biggles untied the painter and picked up the oars – such as they were. The boat surged out on the placid water, leaving its owner raging on the bank.

'This is better,' declared Algy. 'I always did prefer to do my travelling sitting down.'

'You can have a turn at the oars in a minute,' grunted Biggles. 'You won't find that so funny. They're as heavy as a couple of barge sweeps, and the boat feels as if it had a ton of bricks hanging on the bottom.'

'How far is it across the lake, d'you know?' asked Algy.

'You must have seen it from the air.'

'I've seen hundreds of lakes from the air – which one is this?'

'I think I know. I reckon it's about two to three miles across, which should help us a lot, assuming that there isn't another boat in which the Russians can follow us. They'll have to make a detour of seven or eight miles to get round to the far side.'

'By the time we get home we shall have employed pretty nearly all the methods of locomotion known to mankind,' grinned Ginger. 'If we could finish up on roller skates we ought to be able to claim the record. When should we get to the frontier?'

'If we can average three miles an hour, in about six hours,' replied Biggles. 'It can't be more than twenty miles – I fancy it's rather less.'

The boat surged on across the water making a wide ripple on its tranquil surface. The only sound was the soft splash of the oars and the gurgle of the wake.

Presently Algy looked down. 'Great Caesar!' he ejaculated. 'I thought my feet felt cold. Water's coming in somewhere.'

'I'm not surprised at that,' answered Biggles. 'The thing is only tacked together with bits of wire. Look for a bailer – there ought to be one.'

'I can't find one,' muttered Algy, a tinge of alarm creeping into his voice.

'Then use your hat.'

Algy was, in fact, still wearing his flying cap with the earflaps rolled up. 'My hat! That's a bit thick,' he grumbled. However, he took it off and started bailing out the water.

The boat forged on. In front and behind the land showed only as a dark grey shadow.

CHAPTER XIV

Slow Progress

In spite of Algy's efforts more and more water seeped into the boat. Ginger joined in the work of bailing, and although the ingress of water was very slight it still gained on them.

'Can't you pull a bit harder, Biggles?' pleaded Algy, staring at the still distant shore. 'The idea of swimming in this perishing water gives me the horrors.'

'You wouldn't swim very far in it,' returned Biggles. 'You'd be frozen. Here, take a turn at the oars.'

They changed places, and while Biggles bailed, Algy threw all his energy into the rowing. For a while the boat made better progress, but Algy soon used up all his strength, after which the pace became slower than ever. Biggles returned to the oars.

'Either we're going slower than I imagined or else the lake is wider than I thought,' he remarked. 'We don't seem to be getting anywhere.'

'It's probably a bit of both,' put in Ginger.

'We've got to get to the other side before daybreak, that's certain, or we shall be seen by everyone from one end of the lake to the other,' declared Biggles.

In spite of all they could do, and they worked fever-ishly, the water in the boat rose still higher, and it soon became clear that, far from reaching the bank before dawn, they would be lucky to reach it at all. Biggles's efforts at the oars became desperate, for as the boat filled it became more and more sluggish. At last grey light began to steal up from the eastern horizon, and it revealed something that they had not suspected. For some time past Biggles had noticed a piece of land which, from its more definite outline, appeared to be closer than the rest, and taking it to be a promontory, he had pulled towards it. But in the growing light he now saw that it was not a promontory but an island. It was quite small, embracing perhaps two acres of ground, covered for the most part with bulrushes, but with a clump of trees at one end. This suited them nearly as well, if only because it would enable them to rest and empty the water out of the boat, and so make a fresh start; and for this reason Biggles put his last ounce of strength into the task of reaching it before the boat sank under them.

It was touch and go. Ginger and Algy bailed for all they were worth and Biggles pulled as hard as he dared, but he had to be careful, for the gunwales were only a few inches above water. As the keel touched the shelving bottom Biggles called to the others to follow him, and stepping out, he hauled the boat up as far as he could. As soon as its safety was assured they tilted it on its side and so got rid of the water, after which it was an easy matter to pull it up high and dry.

'Phew!' gasped Biggles as he made the boat fast. 'That was a close thing. We'd better get under cover or we may be seen from the shore.'

Three wet, cold, and hungry airmen made their way to the stunted pines that crowded together at the far end of the islet.

'D'you know,' murmured Algy sadly, 'I remember the time when I used to do this sort of thing for fun. We called it a picnic.'

'Don't grumble – we were lucky to get here,' Biggles pointed out. 'How far do you think we are from the shore?'

'Half a mile.'

'At least,' put in Ginger. 'Hadn't we better push on?'

'We might, but it would be dangerous,' answered Biggles. 'We don't know who's about, and it's light enough for anyone on the bank to see us. There's always a risk of an aircraft coming over, too, and then we should be in a mess. Our safest course would be to lie low here until it gets dark before we go on.'

'It's going to be a miserable business sitting here all day with nothing to eat.'

'It would be a still more miserable business sitting in a Russian prison waiting for a firing party to arrive,' said Biggles quietly. 'We've nothing to grumble about.'

From the shelter of the trees they surveyed the mainland, but they could see no movement of any sort apart from a few water-fowl. As the day wore on the sun broke through the clouds; there was little warmth in it, but it made the place look more cheerful, and their spirits rose accordingly. They smiled as they looked at each other. Dirty, unshaven, dishevelled, they were, as Biggles said, a pretty lot of scarecrows. Just before noon an aircraft could be heard, and shortly afterwards a Russian bomber went over, flying very low and steering an erratic course.

'What does he think he's doing?' asked Algy curiously.

'Looking for us, I should say,' replied Biggles laconically. Presently another bomber appeared farther to the north, and yet another, a mere speck in the southern sky.

'If they are looking for us, how do they know about us so soon?' queried Algy.

'Ask me something easier. Perhaps the crowd von Stalhein was with had a portable wireless transmitter. Most modern armies carry radio equipment.'

'What could they do if they spotted us?'

'They might bomb us.'

'Or machine-gun us,' put in Ginger.

'And don't forget that the Russians specialise in parachute units,' reminded Biggles. 'We've already seen an example of that. There might be a score or more of men in each of those machines ready to jump on us the moment they saw us.'

'That's cheerful, I must say,' murmured Algy.

'Well, you asked for it.'

The bombers disappeared towards the west, and for a little while there was silence; then a hail floated over the water. It brought the castaways round with a rush, facing the direction from which it had come.

'Take a look at that,' whispered Algy hoarsely, pointing to the northern end of the distant shore.

The others looked, and saw a large body of Russian troops moving along the bank. Some followed the water's edge, others kept to the higher ground.

'Looks like the crowd von Stalhein was with,' remarked Biggles calmly. 'It's a pity they've got between us and home, but it couldn't be prevented.'

For a long time they lay and watched the soldiers, who, after marching for some distance down the bank, disappeared into the forest in a westerly direction.

'They're going to patrol the frontier, I guess,' said Algy.

'That's about it,' replied Biggles. 'No matter,' he added smiling, 'it will add zest to our homeward trek.'

'Zest, eh?' snorted Algy. 'Hullo, what's this coming? It must be one of the bombers coming back – but it doesn't look like one of those that went over.'

The aircraft was as yet a speck in the sky, flying fast and very low, but as it drew nearer Biggles sprang to his feet. 'By glory!' he cried, 'it's one of ours!'

'You mean a Finn?' Algy asked the question.

'No, British. Look, you can see the markings. It's a Short flying-boat.'

'But what on earth—'

'It's looking for us. Smyth must be flying it.'

'But where the dickens did he get it?'

'I should say there's only one answer to that question. Colonel Raymond, as soon as he realised that the ice had melted, must have radioed for one as the only means of getting us home. He would guess how we'd be stuck when the thaw came.'

The flying-boat roared over the lake about a mile to the south of the island, too far away for there to be any chance of the pilot seeing them. Algy wanted to light a fire, but Biggles forbade it.

'To start with,' he asserted, 'it's by no means sure that the pilot would see the smoke – he's already gone too far over. Secondly, if he did, there is no reason why he should suppose it was us. And thirdly, we've no guarantee that there are no Russians within sight of the lake. They'd spot the smoke, and they'd soon be over to investigate. We should look fools then, shouldn't we?'

The flying-boat roared straight on and soon disappeared in the eastern sky.

'But if it's looking for us why didn't the pilot circle round?' argued Algy.

'Obviously, because it didn't occur to him that we might be so near the frontier. After all, why should it? He's going on to the lake where we crashed the Blenheim. Naturally, that's where he'd expect to find us.'

'That's a bit thick,' muttered Ginger. 'Had we stayed where we were we should have been all right.'

'I agree it is maddening, but "ifs" don't count in this game,' was Biggles's last observation on the matter.

A little while later two Messerschmitts passed over the lake, some distance to the north, and shortly afterwards the Russian bombers came back.

'Great Scott! The sky is absolutely stiff with machines,' declared Algy.

'Yes, we've certainly stirred things up,' agreed Biggles smiling. He glanced at the sun, now far down in the west. Twilight was beginning to settle over the inhospitable land. 'We haven't much longer to wait,' he added. 'As soon as the sun goes down we'll be on our way.'

Nothing more was said. The aircraft disappeared like birds going home to roost. Silence returned. There was no sign of the Russians on the distant shore, and Biggles was justified in hoping that they had left the vicinity. The others were now impatient to be off, but Biggles was too wise to take unnecessary risks by making a premature start. He insisted on waiting until the sun sank behind the hills and darkness fell. As far as they could see there was no sign of human occupation, in all the surrounding landscape.

They launched the boat quietly and took their places. Biggles picked up the oars. He was beginning to feel weak from want of food, but he said nothing about it, and the boat, now free of water, made good progress. Nearing the land he began to proceed with more caution. 'Keep your eyes skinned,' he warned the others. 'If you see anything suspicious let me know; otherwise keep quiet.'

It was a tense moment as the boat crept up to the silent shore; they had no proof that they had not been seen, and for all they knew a score of Russian rifles might be waiting to receive them. Water was gurgling softly in the bottom of the boat, but none of them noticed it; they were too intent on what they were doing. At a distance of twenty yards Biggles turned the boat about and backed in, very slowly, ready to pull out again the instant danger threatened; but nothing happened, so he shipped the oars and allowed the little craft to glide on. It came to rest under the bank. For a minute they all sat still, nerves strained to catch the slightest sound. Then Biggles got out. 'I think it's all right,' he said softly.

Hardly had the words left his lips when voices could be heard approaching. Biggles crouched flat against the muddy bank; the others remained in the boat which Algy, by pulling on a root, drew right in flush with the bank.

How many men there were in the party that came along the lakeside they did not know; nor could they see who they were. They spoke – indeed they seemed to be talking excitedly; but what they said was unintelligible; presumably they were talking in Russian. They crashed along, making a good deal of noise. Once they stopped and were silent. It was a nasty moment for the fugitives. But then the conversation was resumed; brushwood crashed and the footsteps receded. Presently the sounds died away in the distance.

Biggles wiped his forehead. 'This is making an old man of me,' he breathed. 'For the love of Mike don't make a noise – it looks as if the whole blessed country is swarming with Russians. That must have been a patrol just gone past.

All right, come on. Leave the boat under the bushes where it won't be seen in the morning.'

Presently the others joined him. For a little while they stood motionless, listening.

'Single file, but keep close together. Stop if I stop,' whispered Biggles.

In front of them the ground rose steeply. What lay beyond the ridge none of them knew, but their way lay in that direction so they took it unhesitatingly. Biggles led. They crept up the slope, stopping every few minutes to listen. At length, moving like shadows, they breasted the ridge and looked over. Beyond, the ground fell away into vague mysterious shadows, which they could only assume was rugged country similar to that which they had crossed on the far side of the lake. Straight in front, on the line they would have to take, a dim light could be observed. It did not move, and appeared to be shining from the window of a dwelling-house. Biggles glanced at the heavens, picked out a star to guide him on a straight course, and resumed the march.

For an hour they went on steadily, not relaxing their caution, and still halting frequently to listen. Once, in the distance, they heard a sound like someone chopping wood with an axe; on another occasion a wolf howled. That was all. Progress in these circumstances was, of course, slow, and Biggles reckoned that they had covered about a mile, which was not unsatisfactory, for they still had several hours of darkness before them, and he felt that if they could keep up the same pace dawn ought to see them very close to the frontier.

During one of the frequent halts Ginger whispered to Biggles, 'We didn't see the flying-boat come back.'

'It may be staying the night on the lake, or, what is more likely, it went home by a different route,' answered Biggles softly, and then went on again.

In front of them the light, which they now saw came from a window of a substantial house, glowed ever more strongly, and it became clear that if they held on their present course they would pass within a short distance of it. Biggles, however, had no intention of doing this, so he began to edge away to the right in order to miss it by a fairly wide margin. He knew that at such a lonely residence there would certainly be a dog, perhaps several, and not lap-dogs either, but the big husky wolfhound type of animal common in northern Europe – a house-dog in the true sense of the word. Apart from the risk of being attacked and perhaps badly bitten, if they passed too near the house the dog's keen ears would detect them, with the result that there would be a commotion. So he decided to steer clear.

Then, suddenly, the light went out.

'What does that mean?' whispered Algy.

'I should say it means that the people have gone to bed,' answered Biggles without stopping.

As they drew level with it, at a distance of some two hundred yards, it was possible to see the building silhouetted against the sky, for it stood on high ground, and it turned out to be a much larger establishment than they had at first supposed.

It put an idea into Ginger's head. He was hungry, very hungry; indeed, he was weak from hunger. In fact, they were all feeling the strain, although none would be the first to admit it. Biggles's wounded head was beginning to throb again; he was exhausted, and only forced himself to continue the march by sheer willpower.

'I wonder if we could get any food from that place?' whispered Ginger.

Biggles halted and then sat down. 'Let's rest for a minute,' he suggested.

Algy glanced at Ginger and made a grimace. It was unlike Biggles to suggest a rest, and he guessed the reason – that he was very near the end of his strength. He himself was feeling anything but bright, for he had been more badly bruised and shaken by his crash than he admitted. He sat down near Biggles.

Ginger looked at both of them. 'There was a time years ago, before you found me wandering about without visible means of subsistence, when I was pretty good at foraging for food,' he said quietly. 'We need food badly.'

'We can do without it,' said Biggles in a hard voice. 'We're too near the frontier to take risks.'

'That may be so, but we've got twenty miles to go after we cross before we can hope to find food, don't forget. Remember what happened to the professor – he was wandering about for days without finding help.'

'The weather conditions were worse then,' argued Biggles obstinately.

'Food, even a few raw potatoes, would put new life in us,' persisted Ginger.

'Listen, laddie,' said Biggles tersely. 'I know something about this escape business. In nine cases out of ten, when fellows are caught they slip up in the same way. They get desperate for food, and give themselves away trying to get it.'

'Well, I can understand that,' agreed Ginger.

'You're suggesting that we make the same blunder.'

'You think we can last three or four more days without food? It can hardly be less, and it might even be longer.'

Biggles hesitated. The truth of Ginger's argument was not to be denied, and he realised that none of them could go on much longer without food and not crack up. 'What d'you suggest?' he asked.

'I suggest that you two stay here while I have a scout round the house. I won't take any risks. A place that size ought to have outbuildings, and there should be food stored in them, if only field crops. Cut off as they are from anywhere, the people here would be certain to have enough food to last them through the winter.'

Biggles looked at Algy. 'What d'you think?'

'Well, I think it's a risk, but there's no doubt that we need food badly; in fact, if we don't soon get some there seems to be a serious risk of our passing out from sheer starvation. In any case, unless we get some food we shall be too weak to put up any sort of resistance if we happen to run into a bunch of Russians. We should be more in the mood to give ourselves up – if only for the sake of getting something to eat.'

'The danger is dogs.'

Algy shrugged his shoulders. 'Of course – but there it is. It's up to you to decide if the risk is worthwhile.'

Biggles turned to Ginger. 'All right,' he said slowly. 'Have a shot at it, laddie, but for the love of Mike be careful. If a dog starts barking come straight back here and we'll push on.'

Ginger smiled. 'I'll be careful,' he said, and disappeared into the gloom.

CHAPTER XV

A Staggering Discovery

Never had Ginger approached a project with such excessive caution as he now employed; the need for it could hardly be exaggerated, for it seemed highly probable that on his success or failure the lives of all of them depended. When he had promised to take no risks he had meant it, but he knew that the whole enterprise was a risk, a ghastly risk. Still, it was a risk that had to be taken if they were to avoid the greater risk of dying of starvation, or sinking into such a low condition that they would be unequal to the task before them. No felon engaged in a nefarious operation ever approached an object with greater stealth than he observed in his advance upon the lonely dwelling that loomed like a great black shadow in front of him. Without giving the matter any serious thought, he had assumed it to be the residence of the local landowner, a prosperous farmer, or, as we might say, the lord of the manor, and it was not until he drew close that he realised that it was something even larger. It could nearly lay claim to the title of castle. In the days before the revolution it must have been the country seat of some noble family.

The building stood in the centre of what had once doubtless been extensive gardens, the whole surrounded by trees, many of them ornamental evergreens that had obviously been imported; but the gardens were now a jungle, and a tangle of briars and bushes, brown and sere from the icy grip of winter, had advanced almost to the walls. This undergrowth offered a certain amount of cover, an advantage that was largely offset, however, by its liability to snap when trodden on.

The building itself was in a bad state of repair, and presented a woebegone appearance. All this Ginger noted as he stood on the inner edge of the encircling belt of trees. Motionless as a statue, he surveyed the structure section by section, window by window, making a picture in his mind of the most salient features, and noting particularly such windows on the ground floor as might lend themselves to his purpose. And as he stood there a chain rattled, a harsh metallic jangle, somewhere at the rear of the house. His eyes flashed to the spot and he perceived a group of outbuildings. The sound furnished him with a useful piece of information; it told him that a dog was there. It also told him that the dog was chained up. He could judge pretty well where it was, so he made a mental note to avoid the spot. It was for this reason that he first turned his attention to the front of the house.

Slowly, exploring the ground with his feet for twigs before putting his weight down, he went on, and presently stood close against the wall. All was silent, as, indeed, was only to be expected, for the hour was late, and it was reasonable to suppose that the occupants of the house were in bed. Had it not been for the lighted window, which proved conclusively that somebody was inside, he would have thought that the house was deserted. Unhurriedly, eyes and ears alert, keeping close against the wall, he moved across the front of the house, trying the front door

– a massive portal – on the way. It was locked. He went on to the far corner, and then stopped suddenly, his heart beating faster. Faintly to his ears came the sound of voices, and peering round the corner he made a discovery for which he was not prepared. The light that they had seen as they approached the house must, he now realised, have been in one of the front windows, for the house faced in that direction; and when this light had been extinguished he had supposed, not unnaturally, that the household had retired. But from the corner where he now stood he was able to look along the side of the house farthest from their line of approach – that is to say, farthest from the place where the others were now waiting for him – and to his surprise he perceived that someone was still about, and, moreover, on the ground floor. A shaft of pale orange light issued from a window and fell across the tangle of shrubs outside. Advancing a few more paces, he saw that the window was curtained; the curtains had been drawn, but as they did not meet in the middle a narrow space was left uncovered, and it was from this that the light proceeded.

This at once altered Ginger's plan. He had intended to explore the ground floor for the kitchen, and with everyone upstairs he had imagined that this would be no difficult matter; but if people were still downstairs it would be extremely risky. The kitchen of course would be at the back of the house, but he had avoided making an entry from the rear on account of the dog. Now he hardly knew what to do for the best, but after giving the matter some thought he decided first of all to take a peep through the window in order to see who it was with whom he had to deal, and with this object in view he moved on down the wall towards it.

As he drew nearer to it the sound of voices increased in volume. Then words reached his ears that stunned him into immobility, for they were spoken in English. This, he told himself, was past belief. He expected the conversation would be in Russian. He would not have been surprised had it been in German, or Finnish, or any Scandinavian tongue; but English! Who in the name of heaven could be talking English in such a place? Surely he had been mistaken – his ears had deceived him. But then he distinctly heard a man say, 'Very good.' And at the sound of that voice his lips turned dry. He crept on and looked through the window.

In his life Ginger had had many shocks, but never one such as he now received. His nerves all seemed to tighten like elastic, causing the sensation known as pins and needles to prickle his skin. For this is what he saw.

There were five people in the room, seated round a large table on which still rested the remains of a substantial meal. Three of the men were Russian officers; another was von Stalhein, although Ginger was not particularly surprised at that, for the German had doubtless been with the Russians who had circumnavigated the lake while they had been rowing across it, and had later gone on towards the frontier. This house had apparently been his objective. It was the presence of the fifth man that numbed Ginger with shock. He knew him only slightly, but he had seen him many times; in fact the man had more than once endeavoured to engage him in conversation, but he was a type that repelled rather than attracted him, and the acquaintanceship had never ripened. He was, in fact, a member of the International Squadron fighting for Finland, a Swede named Olsen who had lived most of his life in Canada – at least, that was what he had said, and this was to some extent borne out by the fact that the only language he spoke was English, and that with a Western accent. Presumably it was for this reason that English was the language employed in the present conversation with von Stalhein – with whom, incidentally, he seemed quite at home.

Ginger listened horrified as he heard the alleged Swede describing in detail the Finnish plans for defence, leaving no doubt whatever that his real business in the Finnish Air Force was that of a spy, acting on behalf of either Germany or Russia. He spoke volubly, while von Stalhein, nodding occasionally, made notes on a sheet of paper. The Russians seemed content to listen. Ginger could hear everything that passed.

When Olsen had finished von Stalhein took several envelopes from his pocket. 'Take these with you when you go back,' he said. 'Deliver them in the usual way. I should like them delivered tomorrow.'

The spy smiled as he took the letters. 'No difficulty about that,' he said.

'You came over in the usual way I suppose?' queried von Stalhein.

'Sure. I'd rather fly than walk. I always leave my crate at the same place – the valley just east of the frontier – and then walk across. By the way, what's going on? The frontier is stiff with troops. If I hadn't known the password I should have been in a mess.'

Von Stalhein sipped his wine, fitted a cigarette into a long holder, and lit it before he replied. 'I've had some trouble,' he said curtly, 'with a fellow named Bigglesworth – you may know him. He's in the International Squadron.'

Olsen started. 'Sure I know the skunk. Because he shot down a few of your crack fliers in the last war he acts like he's running the show.'

Von Stalhein smiled faintly. 'He's a British agent.'

'*What!*' Olsen half rose to his feet. 'Him and them three pals of his always fly as a team. Now you mention it, I ain't seen them for the last day or two. What have they been up to?'

'I wish I had a team like it,' confessed von Stalhein frankly. 'They've been over here and they've got away with some important documents. I have good reason to believe that they're still in Russia, trying to work their way home on foot, having crashed their machines. Hence the troops on the frontier. I'm hoping to catch them when they try to cross.'

Olsen emptied his wineglass. 'Say, what d'you know about that!' he exclaimed. 'Why didn't you grab him before?'

Again a suspicion of a smile crossed the German's austere face. 'Have you ever tried to grab a live eel with your bare hands?'

'Aw shucks! He can't be that clever.'

Von Stalhein leaned forward in his chair. 'Would you like to have a shot at catching him?'

Olsen winked. 'Why not? What's it worth if I do it?'

The German's manner became crisp. 'I'll tell you what I'll do,' he said. 'As I told you, I'm trying to catch Bigglesworth and his friends myself, and it's probable that I shall; but should he slip through my fingers – and he's got a trick of doing that – he'll make straight for Oskar to hand the papers over to his employers. Bring those papers back to me and I'll pay you a thousand pounds. I'll pay you another thousand for Bigglesworth, dead or alive, and five hundred for each of the others.'

The spy grinned delightedly. 'That sure sounds like easy money to me,' he declared. 'Next time I come over they'll be with me – dead or alive. Come to think of it, though, they'd make rather a heavy load for a single-seater. Would the heads be enough?'

Von Stalhein frowned. He looked disgusted. 'Olsen, I fancy you are living about four centuries too late.'

'War's war, ain't it? I ain't squeamish.'

'So I observe,' returned von Stalhein drily. 'Very well, we'll dispense with the bodies. I'll pay for the heads. But be careful you aren't suspected.'

'Me? Suspected? Why, the Finns reckon I'm as good a Swede as ever came out of Sweden.'

Von Stalhein made some notes and handed the paper to one of the Russian officers, with whom he conversed for some minutes in his own language. Then they all finished their wine, got up, pushed their chairs back, and filed out of the room. One of the Russians was the last to leave. He closed the door behind him.

Ginger had had time to recover from his first shock, but as a result of the conversation he had just heard he still felt a trifle dazed. Dazed is perhaps not quite the right word. His brain was racing so fast that he wanted to do several things at once. He wanted to rush into the house and shoot the treacherous spy before he could do further damage. He wanted to rush back to Biggles and acquaint him with the horrid facts. He wanted to tear back to Finland and warn the people there that their plans were known to the enemy; and he wanted to fulfil the original object of his expedition, which was to get some food, plenty of which remained on the table within a few feet of him. The temptation to get some of it was too great to be resisted; he felt that it would make such a difference to them if he could get even a little food, and he made up his mind to try.

With this object in view he attempted to open the window. It was fastened. For a moment he was dismayed, but only for a moment. The panes were small and lead-framed, and the lead being of great age, it had weathered to the thinness of paper. He found a loose pane near the inside catch and prized away the lead until he could remove the glass intact. Having disposed of this, he put a hand through the aperture thus made and slipped the catch. In a minute the window was open and he was inside. Leaving the window open and the curtains drawn ready for a quick evacuation should it become necessary, he went straight to the table, for nothing else interested him. Half a roast chicken looked tempting, as did the carcass of a goose. He gathered together several large pieces of bread, and was making ready to depart when he saw a dish in which still remained a number of baked potatoes. The question was, how to carry them? A napkin answered it. He opened it out flat, and was about to empty the dish into it when a sound from the direction of the window brought him round with a jerk. A hairy face above a Russian uniform grinned at him. A bando-lier crossed the man's chest, and a rifle hung by its sling from his shoulder. Obviously he was a sentry. To Ginger's consternation, he crawled clumsily over the windowsill and stood just inside, still grinning amiably and pointing at the table.

At first Ginger could not get the hang of such peculiar behaviour. Then, suddenly, he understood. The fellow took him for one of the servants, and supposed that he was clearing the table. The question was how to get rid of him. On the table stood several long-necked wine bottles. Ginger tried two or three in quick succession, but they were all empty; then he found one that was still half full. He held it up to the man, at the same time raising his eyebrows questioningly above a rather nervous smile.

The man said something – what it was Ginger had no idea – and held out his hand for the bottle. Ginger crossed the room swiftly and gave it to him, and then tapped him on the shoulder with a gesture which he hoped would convey the impression that instant departure would be appreciated. The man understood. He stuffed the bottle inside the breast of his greatcoat, said something, and went off – still grinning.

Ginger's relief was such that he nearly collapsed, but he had no intention of leaving the food. He crept back to the table and gathered it up. The bread he stuffed into his pockets. Nor did he leave the potatoes. He emptied the lot into the napkin, caught up the corners, and with the skeleton of the goose under his arm, the chicken in one hand and the napkin in the other, he returned swiftly to the window. He was only just in time, for footsteps could be heard approaching.

He was outside and in the act of closing the window when the door opened and a servant came into the room. However, the man appeared to see nothing unusual, for he started collecting the dishes. Ginger paid no further attention to the window. Picking up his loot, he took one quick look round for the sentry, and not seeing him, stepped stealthily into the cover of the trees, like a fox departing from a plundered farmyard.

Now that he had reached comparative safety his reaction following the last few hectic minutes was so intense that his legs nearly gave way under him, and he had to rest for a moment to recover his composure; then, happy in the knowledge of the success of his mission, and the tremendous information he had to impart, he sped on. He fairly staggered to the place where the others were waiting.

'Sweet spirit of Icarus! What's he got?' gasped Algy.

Ginger thrust the goose carcass into his hands. 'Hold that,' he panted. He held out the chicken to Biggles. 'Lay hold,' he implored him. 'Let's get away from here. I've got news for you that will make you jump.'

'You've got some grub, and that's enough to make me break any jumping record, without anything else,' declared Algy emphatically.

'Don't you believe it,' said Ginger in a voice vibrant with emotion.

'What is it – is von Stalhein in there?' guessed Biggles shrewdly.

'You bet your life he is, and that's not half of it,' panted Ginger. 'Here we are, this will do.' He led the way into a small gully between some rocks. 'Now get an earful of this,' he continued tersely, and forthwith in as few words as possible related what had transpired at the house.

'Good work, laddie,' said Biggles when he had finished. 'It seems that von Stalhein is a bigger skunk than I thought, to put a price on our heads; but as for that foul traitor, Olsen, hanging would be too good for him. There are moments when I regret that torture has gone out of fashion, and this is one of them. Once or twice we've had to sail near the wind in this spy business ourselves, but we don't stoop to murder. Nor do we line our pockets with dirty money. We'd better not stop to eat here. We've got to get Olsen. He knows the password, and if for no other reason we've got to intercept him. If we know what it is—'

'You don't suppose he'll tell you, do you?' broke in Algy.

'Won't he!' The others had never heard Biggles's voice so hard. 'By the time I've finished with that skunk he'll be ready to tell anything, I'll warrant,' he continued. 'There must be a path running westwards from the house, leading to the frontier – unless Olsen walked across country, which doesn't seem feasible. There's bound to be a drive of some sort leading to a house of this size, and since it isn't on this side it must be on the other. If we strike straight across the rear of the building we should come to it. Let's go.'

Biggles set off, still carrying the chicken; the others followed close behind. Over rocks, through bushes, between trees where it was nearly pitch dark, and even across a watercourse, they pushed on until at length, as Biggles had surmised, they struck a track which clearly led to the house. They came upon it at a distance of rather less than a quarter of a mile from the building itself, and Biggles reconnoitred in both directions before he stepped onto it. 'All clear,' he said. 'This must be it. The track should run straight from the house to the frontier, and unless I'm mistaken Olsen will walk down it on his way back. We'll wait for him here; we shan't find anything better suited to our purpose.'

At this point the track, which had a terrible surface but was wide enough for a wheeled vehicle, ran through a shallow gully, with tall trees on either side.

'We can wait, listen, and eat at the same time,' said Biggles, mustering the food.

Algy clicked his tongue when he saw the bread and potatoes. 'This exceeds my wildest hopes,' he announced in a voice heavy with satisfaction.

'I should think it jolly well does,' returned Biggles. 'I thought we should do well if we got a few raw potatoes, but roast chicken, roast goose, potatoes, and bread – Ginger, you're a wizard.' With scant ceremony Biggles divided the food, tearing the remains of the two birds apart with his hands. Real hunger makes short work of conventional politeness. 'No more talking,' warned Biggles. 'We've got to listen. Eat fast in case he comes.'

'You're telling me,' grunted Algy, tearing at a goose leg with his teeth.

For ten minutes nothing could be heard but the steady munch of jaws, and by the end of that time every scrap of Ginger's haul, with the exception of a few bones, had disappeared.

Algy wiped his fingers on his trousers. 'By James! That's better,' he breathed.

The others smiled but said nothing. They found comfortable positions just inside the trees. Biggles took out his gun, and Algy, with the rifle across his knees, sat down to wait.

CHAPTER XVI

A Desperate Flight

For the remainder of the night the comrades kept their lonely vigil, and it was not until the eastern sky was turning grey that they heard someone coming from the direction of the house. A stone rattled; footsteps crunched on the rough gravel, and presently Olsen could be seen, a leather flying jacket over his arm and cap and goggles swinging in his left hand, coming down the track.

'Good, he's alone,' whispered Biggles. 'Don't move until I give the word.'

Not until the spy drew level did Biggles stir. Then he got up, and with his hands in his pockets strolled out onto the track.

'Hullo, Olsen,' he said casually, 'what are you doing here?'

Olsen sprang back as if he had been struck. For a moment he looked confused, but then, with what must have been a tremendous effort, he recovered himself. But his face had turned pale, and his eyes flashed round as if seeking to ascertain whether Biggles was alone.

'Why – I – er – I had a forced landing,' he stammered.

'In that case, aren't you taking a bit of a risk, strolling about like this in a hostile country as if the place belonged to you?'

'What are you doing here, if it comes to that?' asked Olsen belligerently.

'Oh, I had a bit of business to transact.'

'Is that so?'

'Yes, that is so – but not your sort of business.'

Olsen's right hand was creeping towards his pocket.

'I shouldn't try that if I were you,' resumed Biggles quietly. 'Right now there's a rifle pointing straight at you, and I don't think it would require much excuse to make Algy Lacey pull the trigger.' Biggles's voice hardened. 'It's no use, Olsen. We know your business.'

Olsen blustered. 'What are you talking about?'

'You know what we're talking about. You were a trifle premature selling our heads to von Stalhein. I'm thinking of sending yours to him instead. Hand over those letters.'

'Letters – what letters?'

Biggles drew his pistol, and without turning addressed the others. 'You can come out,' he ordered. 'Algy, take that gun out of Olsen's pocket – and the letters. Put your hands up, Olsen – and keep them up. I'm giving you better treatment than you deserve, so don't try any funny stuff. It wouldn't take much to make me change my mind.'

Olsen, as white as death, his nostrils distended and the corners of his mouth dragged down with rage and fear, slowly raised his hands. Algy took a revolver from his side pocket, and the letters. The revolver he passed to Ginger.

'Olsen,' continued Biggles, 'there are moments when I am tempted to commit murder, and this is one of them, but against my inclination I'm going to take you back to Finland for a fair trial. We've got to get through the Russian lines. You know the password. What is it?'

Olsen shrugged his shoulders. 'How should I know?'

Biggles showed his teeth in a mirthless smile. 'There's a good reason why you should know, and you know that, so we needn't discuss it. It happens that your conversation last night was overheard. I've no time to waste talking. What's the password? Say you don't know again and I shall no longer have any reason for keeping you alive, so make up your mind.'

The spy looked at the three faces that confronted him. They were grim and hostile. There was no mercy in the accusing eyes. Nobody knew better than he the extent of his guilt, and he knew what he would have done had the position been reversed. Possibly it was this knowledge that made him weaken.

'Okay,' he said slowly, 'I guess you've got the works on me. If I tell you, will you let me go?'

'No, by thunder, I won't,' flashed back Biggles harshly. 'You're coming with us. If we run into any Russians, and you make one false move, I shall fire the first shot, and it will be at you. So make up your mind to it, Olsen; whatever happens you're not going to get away to go on with this dirty work. You can tell us the password and come with us, or keep your mouth shut and take what's coming to you.' Biggles raised his pistol.

Olsen shrank back. 'No – don't do that,' he faltered, white-lipped. 'The password's "Petrovith".'

'For your own sake I hope you're not lying,' said Biggles evenly. 'All right – let's go.'

He inspected the track in the direction of the house, and then pointed down it towards the frontier with his pistol.

The party moved off, Olsen walking in front with Biggles's pistol pointing at his back, and in this manner they proceeded for some distance. Then, without warning, a shout rang through the air.

Biggles sprang round. The others did the same. It was now light enough for them to see for some distance, light enough to reveal a startling picture. Just emerging out of the thin veil of mist that clung to the top of the hill on which the house was situated was a party of Russian soldiers. That they had seen the fugitives was at once obvious from their attitudes.

Of the four who stood on the track Olsen was the first to move, and he moved like lightning. He gave Biggles a violent shove, and then, ducking low, and twisting as he ran, he dashed towards the Russians.

Biggles steadied himself. War was war, and he had no intention of allowing the spy to escape; he owed it to the Finns whom Olsen had betrayed, quite apart from the man's promise to von Stalhein that he would bring him their heads. He shouted to Olsen to stop, or he would shoot. Olsen's answer was to whip out a small automatic from under his arm and let drive. Biggles jumped aside the instant he saw the weapon and the bullet whistled past his head. He threw up his own weapon, took deliberate aim and fired. Olsen staggered; his knees crumpled under him and he sprawled face downwards across the track.

By this time the Russians were within two hundred yards and running towards the spot. Biggles thrust the weapon in his pocket, and shouting 'This way!' dashed off through the trees. The others followed.

Now although the Russians were so close, the comrades had this advantage: once within the trees they could not be seen, so it would not be known what direction they had taken. At first Biggles chose the easiest way, for his paramount thought was to put as much ground as possible between him and the Russians, for he realised that, now it was known definitely that they were still inside the frontier, it would only be a question of time before all the troops in the vicinity would join in the hunt, and by that time the password would be useless. After his first spurt, therefore, he turned in a westerly direction, hoping to reach the frontier before the news of their escape was known; if they could do that there was still a chance that they could bluff their way through on the strength of the password. So, still heading west, he pressed on at top speed until the edge of the wood revealed itself ahead. The trees did not end abruptly, but first began to stand farther apart; they then straggled out over country more in the nature of open heath. Between the trees lay dense growths of bracken, gorse, and heather, brown from the winter frosts.

Reaching this open country, Biggles pulled up for a moment and made a swift reconnaissance, which he was well able to do by virtue of the fact that the ground fell away in a slope, sometimes gentle and sometimes steep, for a considerable distance. Here and there grey rocks, rising to some height, broke through the undergrowth, and towards the nearest of these Biggles made his way.

'Keep your eyes open,' he told the others, and then scrambled up the rock. For a few moments he lay flat, his eyes exploring the scene ahead; then he slid back to the ground.

'There are troops all over the place,' he said quietly. 'We must be very close to the frontier even if we're not already on it, although I can't see any sign of the actual boundary. All we can do is to go on; we'll avoid the troops if we can, but if we're accosted we'll give the password and hope for the best. I can see the track Olsen was following – at least, I can see a track, and it's hardly likely that there are two. It disappears into a forest about a mile ahead. We'll make for the forest and march parallel with the track in the hope of finding Olsen's machine – he would be bound to land as near the track as possible.'

'Lead on,' said Algy briefly.

Progress was now slower, for while crossing the open country it was necessary to scout every inch of the way. Several times they passed close to small detachments of Russian soldiers, and once they had to lie flat while a patrol went past within fifty yards of them. However, they moved steadily nearer to their objective, and they had in fact almost reached it when suddenly and unexpectedly they came upon two soldiers sitting smoking near an outcrop of rock. The Russians saw them at once and jumped to their feet.

Biggles, looking as unconcerned as possible, went straight to them and announced the password. He was anxious to avoid hostilities if it were possible. It was a nasty moment, for up to that time they had no means of knowing if Olsen had told the truth; but it was soon obvious that the password was the correct one. Nevertheless, the Russians seemed somewhat mystified and held a low conversation, whereupon Biggles took the letters from his pocket – the letters which he had taken from Olsen – and after pointing to the addresses, he nodded towards the west in the hope that the two simple fellows would grasp what he was trying to convey – that the letters had to be delivered. This seemed to satisfy the Russians, who made a joke of the travellers' unkempt appearance, apparently under the impression that this was a disguise, and indicated that they might proceed. They needed no second invitation.

Their relief at this simple evasion was short-lived, however, for they had not gone very far when Biggles, happening to look behind, saw the same two Russians coming after them at a run; following them were several more.

Biggles instantly grasped what had happened. The newcomers had brought news of their escape, with a result that the complacent soldiers were now hastening to rectify their mistake. The position was desperate, but Biggles did not lose his head; he maintained the same pace and the same unconcerned attitude until he reached the trees, knowing that if he started to run the Russians would shoot. As he went on he told the others what had happened. But as soon as they were under cover inside the trees he broke into a sprint, striking diagonally through the forest in order to reach the track, the position of which he still carried in his mind.

'Are we over the frontier yet?' panted Algy, as they dashed between the sombre pines.

'I don't know,' answered Biggles. 'It's hard to say. Not that the actual frontier counts for much now there's a war on. The only real advantage of being in Finland is that we might strike a patrol of Finnish troops.'

As Biggles anticipated, they soon reached the track, but he was not so foolish as to expose himself on it; instead he sped on keeping parallel with it, and just within sight of it. There was little undergrowth beneath the trees, so they were able to travel as fast as if they were actually on the track.

By this time the hue and cry could be heard. Shouts came from several points; whistles blew and shots were fired, although what the Russians were shooting at Biggles could not imagine, for he was positive that they could not be seen. He could only conclude that the troops were firing blindly into the trees in the hope that a lucky shot would halt them.

It was Ginger who spotted the aircraft – a Gladiator carrying Finnish markings. The trees ended abruptly and gave way to a flat, low-lying valley large enough to enable a machine to land. The Gladiator stood close in under the trees, presumably so that it could not be seen from above, and might easily have been passed unnoticed had not they known definitely that an aircraft was in the vicinity.

Now the Gladiator is a single-seater, so it was at once obvious that it offered escape for one only. It did not take Biggles long to decide who it should be.

'You'll fly it, Ginger,' he said as they raced towards it. 'Take the papers and the letters straight to Colonel Raymond at Oskar and tell him what has happened. If he can send help, well and good; otherwise we shall have to go on trying to get home on foot.'

Ginger knew Biggles too well to attempt to argue with him at a time like this. 'Right!' he said, taking the elusive papers, and the letters, and thrusting them into his pocket. He swung up into the cockpit. 'Good luck,' he cried in a strangled voice. The engine started at the second attempt; the propeller flashed, a whirling arc of light, then the Gladiator surged forward and, after bumping once or twice on the uneven ground, roared into the sky.

A babble of voices and the crashing of bushes told Biggles and Algy that their pursuers were closing in on them, so they wasted no time watching the machine. Some distance to the right was one of the many lakes with which the country abounded, and towards this Biggles now led the way. Why he chose the lake he really did not know, unless it was because he felt that the steep, reed-lined banks offered more promise of a hiding-place than the open country. In any case it would have been fatal to attempt to cross the open ground in front of the Russian rifles. He ran straight into the rushes until he was ankle-deep in water, and then started to follow the bank, still heading in a westerly direction. Algy kept close behind him. And they were only just in time taking cover, for hardly had they entered the reeds than a number of Russians appeared on the edge of the forest a hundred yards or so away, where they halted, apparently uncertain which way to take. Curiously enough, the very number of them made matters easier for the airmen, for the Russians had evidently outstripped their officers, and as no one seemed able to keep order, they argued among themselves, each man advocating the direction that made most appeal to him. In this way Biggles and Algy got a fair start, and for a little while it looked as if they might actually get clear away.

But then a new factor appeared on the scene, one that made a lot of difference; it was von Stalhein with two Russian officers, all on horseback, and the German lost no time in organising the pursuit on efficient lines. The troops were formed into detachments, and these were set into motion to sweep the landscape so that no part of it remained unsearched.

It was the bomber that finally located them. Where it suddenly appeared from neither Biggles nor Algy knew, but there was a roar overhead, and then the machine, flying low, swept into sight, quartering the ground like a well-trained hound. It was obvious that in some way von Stalhein had managed to get into touch with the pilot, who had brought his machine to the spot.

Biggles and Algy were now compelled to adopt a slower method of procedure. When the aircraft approached near to them they lay still in the reeds, and only when it was some distance away did they dare to continue their flight.

'We shall have to go faster than this; we've wasted too much time lying still,' said Biggles after a quick reconnaissance through the reeds in the direction of the Russian troops, who he saw were drawing perilously near them. Some were actually beginning to search among the reeds at the point where they had entered them.

Algy glanced up at the bomber; it seemed to be a safe distance away. 'Then let's make a dash for it and try to reach those trees at the far end of the lake,' he suggested.

They were now within sight of the far end of the lake, which was not much more than a quarter of a mile away, and there the ground rose steeply to form one of the many rocky ridges that divided several lakes. Trees clothed the flanks of the ridge, and it seemed reasonable to suppose that if they could reach them the task of their pursuers, including the pilot of the aircraft, would be made much more difficult. Biggles saw the wisdom of Algy's advice, and ducking low, he at once broke into a run. Unfortunately they soon came to a place where for some reason the reeds were very short, too short to afford any real cover. However, they made a dash for it, but hardly were they in the open when the aircraft turned. From the manner in which it suddenly came towards them Biggles knew that the pilot, or a member of the crew, had seen them. Straight over them the bomber roared. A small object detached itself from the bottom of the fuselage; it dropped like a stone and burst with a muffled roar about fifty yards away. A mighty cloud of smoke rose high into the air.

'Smoke-bomb,' snapped Biggles. 'That's to tell the crowd where we are. I only hope that von Stalhein is the first to show up – I've got a little present for him.' Biggles took out his pistol. He still continued to run, but it was now obvious from the clamour that the smoke-bomb had done its work.

'It looks as if this is where we fight it out,' observed Algy calmly, clicking a bullet into the breech of the rifle he still carried. He glanced up, wondering why the bomber had not returned to circle over them, and what he saw brought a wild yell to his lips. 'Look!' he shouted.

The bomber was still there, but it was no longer alone in the air. Dropping on it like a torpedo was a Gladiator, and that was not all. Some distance behind the single-seater, looking strangely out of place, and diving as steeply as it dared, was a flying-boat.

'Ginger must be flying that Gladiator – it couldn't be anyone else,' gasped Biggles. 'He must have spotted the flying-boat and brought it here.'

'We must let them know where we are!' cried Algy in a voice which excitement pitched in a treble key.

'Get up on the bank and try to hold off the Russians with the rifle,' ordered Biggles crisply. 'Concentrate on the horsemen first – they're the biggest danger.'

Algy scrambled up the bank, and throwing himself flat, opened fire. There was no further point in trying to hide.

Biggles tore up a quantity of reeds which, like most of the vegetation, were brown and dry from the recent killing frosts, and throwing them into a pile, put a match to them. A thin column of smoke at once rose into the air. Working with frantic speed, he tore up more and more reeds and flung them on the blaze, torn between attending to his task and watching what was happening in the air, for that something lively was happening was certain. Machine-guns chattered shrilly; bullets punctured the placid surface of the lake, and some even plopped into the mud unpleasantly close to where he stood.

Thrilled, as every airman must be when he watches a combat, he looked up at the machines overhead and took in the situation at a glance. The Gladiator was on the bomber's tail now, its guns stuttering in short, vicious bursts. The bomber was diving steeply, banking first one way and then the other in a desperate but futile effort to escape its more agile adversary. Straight on past the bomber the Gladiator roared, and then after a sharp turn swept up underneath it. Biggles could see the tracer bullets like little white sparks of light raking the bottom of the big black fuselage. A feather of smoke, growing swiftly in size, spurted from the bomber's side, and trailed away behind to mark its erratic course. By this time it was obvious that the pilot of the big machine was concerned only with reaching the ground, and he did in fact succeed in doing so. There was a rush of flame and a splintering crash as the wheels touched the rough turf, and Biggles smiled sympathetically as the pilot and crew jumped out and flung themselves clear. The Gladiator turned away at once, but instead of climbing to a safe height, it began sweeping low over the ground with its guns still going.

'What does the young fool think he's doing?' yelled Biggles.

Algy, from the top of the bank, replied, 'He's driving back the mob on the ground.'

Biggles, running up to the ridge, saw that this was true. He had his pistol ready, but a glance told him that it would not be needed – not yet, at any rate – for those men who were not lying flat on the ground to escape the leaden hail were racing for the cover of the trees. Some distance away a horseman was trying to steady a badly frightened horse.

'That's von Stalhein,' muttered Biggles. 'He must be fairly swallowing his tonsils with rage.' Without waiting for Algy to give his opinion, he ran back to the edge of the water and stood clear in the open, waving his arms to attract the attention of the flying-boat pilot. But a moment later he saw that this was unnecessary, for the aircraft was coming in to land on a course that should end near to where he stood. Its keel cut a line of creamy foam on the smooth water; its engines roared with short, spasmodic bursts of sound. Over it now circled the Gladiator. The flying-boat, no longer airborne, surged on towards the place where Biggles stood, reducing its speed as it neared the land.

'Come on! Let's go out to him!' Biggles flung the words over his shoulder to Algy.

Abandoning their position, they splashed out into the icy water and waded knee-deep towards the aircraft. A side window of the cockpit opened, and Smyth's face appeared. 'Come on, sir!' he shouted.

'Good old Smyth; trust him to be in at the death,' declared Algy. 'That man's a treasure. He doesn't talk much, but he's on the spot when he's wanted.'

With the Gladiator still on guard overhead, Biggles and Algy reached the machine; it rocked as they clambered aboard and sank down, panting with exertion and excitement.

'Okay, Smyth – let her go!' shouted Biggles.

Algy looked at Biggles with affected amazement. 'Don't tell me that we're going to get those perishing papers home at *last*,' he muttered. 'I can't believe it.'

'I imagine Ginger still has the papers in his pocket,' returned Biggles anxiously. 'I wish he'd push on home. If his engine chose this moment to pack up—'

'He'd make a pretty landing and we'd have to start all over again,' jeered Algy. 'Forget it. I'm going home.'

Further conversation was drowned in the roar of the flying-boat's engines as Smyth opened the throttle. The water boiled as the machine swung round to face the longest run the lake provided. Then, majestically, it forged forward, faster and faster, cutting a clean white line across the surface of the lake as it lifted itself slowly from the water. The wake ended abruptly as the keel, after a parting pat, rose clear. The machine turned slowly towards the west.

The Gladiator closed in and took up a position near the wing-tip. Ginger's face could just be seen, grinning. Seeing the others looking at him, he gave the thumbs-up signal, and held the papers for them to see.

Algy turned away. He couldn't bear to watch, for he had a horrible fear that Ginger might drop them overboard, and the bare thought made him shudder. He looked down at the ground and saw that the Russian troops were all converging on one spot. Some of them seemed to be waving to the aircraft; others danced as if in a transport of joy, and one or two threw their hats into the air. He turned an amazed face to Biggles.

'I say, what's going on down there?' he asked in a curious tone of voice. 'From the way those fellows are behaving one would think that they are glad to see us go.'

Biggles, too, looked down. He shook his head. 'I don't understand it either,' he observed. 'They look as if they'd all gone crazy. Maybe they have. There have been times in this affair when I thought I'd go crazy myself.'

Algy nodded. 'It's a funny war,' he remarked philosophically.

Biggles stretched himself out on the floor. 'As far as I'm concerned, it can be any sort of war it likes,' he yawned. 'I'm going to sleep. Wake me when we get home.'

CHAPTER XVII

The End of the Cruise

Two hours later the flying-boat landed on a lake near Oskar. The lake was just beyond the aerodrome, so Ginger in the Gladiator was down first, with the result that when Biggles and Algy stepped ashore, Colonel Raymond, with Ginger, was there to welcome him. He had raced over in a car. As he shook hands with them he smiled, presumably at their appearance, which, after what they had been through, can be better imagined than described.

'You look as though you've had a tough time,' he observed.

'Tough!' Algy laughed sarcastically. 'Oh, no. We got ourselves in this mess just to make it look that way.'

'The main thing is, you've got the papers, sir,' put in Biggles.

'Yes, thanks. Good show.' Then the Colonel looked serious. 'I'm sorry you've had so much trouble,' he said. 'I'd no idea it would turn out to be such a difficult and dangerous business. No matter – all's well that ends well.'

'There were times,' answered Biggles reflectively, 'when it looked like ending badly – for us. We only got away by the skin of our teeth.'

Colonel Raymond patted him affectionately on the shoulder. 'Never mind, you're building up a wonderful reputation in Whitehall,' he said comfortingly. 'You may be sure that you'll get the credit for what you've done when I submit my report. Now go and have a bath and a clean-up. Dinner is on me tonight.'

'Where did you produce that flying-boat from so miraculously?' inquired Biggles.

'Produce it? Why, that's the machine that flew me out from England – how did you think I got here? Your man Smyth knew it was here; when you failed to return he came to me in an awful state and asked me to let him have it. He said he thought he knew where he could find you. He's been in the air ever since – I think he must have flown over half Russia.'

'I spotted him in the distance soon after I took off,' explained Ginger. 'He might have found you without me, but in the circumstances I led him to the spot where I took off. That smoke-bomb so kindly dropped by the gent in the Russian bomber showed us where you were.'

'So that was it,' murmured Biggles. 'I thought something of the sort must have happened.'

'If you like you can all fly home with me tomorrow,' offered Colonel Raymond.

Biggles looked puzzled. 'Home with you? Why home?'

'Well, there isn't much point in staying here any longer, is there?'

'But – what about the war?'

'What war?'

'This war.'

A light of understanding suddenly leapt into the Colonel's eyes. He laughed aloud. 'D'you mean to say you haven't heard?'

'Heard what?' cried Biggles. 'What's the joke?'

'The war's over – at least this one is. Peace was declared between Finland and Russia three hours ago.'

Biggles looked thunderstruck. 'Why, less than three hours ago we were still going hammer and tongs.'

'I know. You must have fired the last shots in the war.'

'So *that's* why the Russians stopped shooting and started cheering instead!' cried Biggles, suddenly under-standing.

The Colonel smiled. 'Of course. Most sensible people would rather cheer than shoot each other. Are you coming home with me?'

Biggles glanced at the others. 'Well, there seems to be nothing more to stay here for so we may as well,' he said. 'There's only one thing.'

'What is it?'

'Don't, if you value my sanity, send us on any more of these wild paper-chases.'

'That won't be necessary, now the papers are in the bag,' laughed Colonel Raymond. 'Come on, let's be going. As a matter of fact, the day I left England I heard a certain member of the Air Council asking for you.'

Biggles looked up. 'Asking for me? What did he want me for?'

Colonel Raymond coughed apologetically. 'Well – er – I seem to remember him saying something about a job in France.'

Biggles shook his head sadly. 'Now I understand the hurry to get us home,' he murmured with a sigh of resig-nation. 'I might have guessed there was a trick in it.'

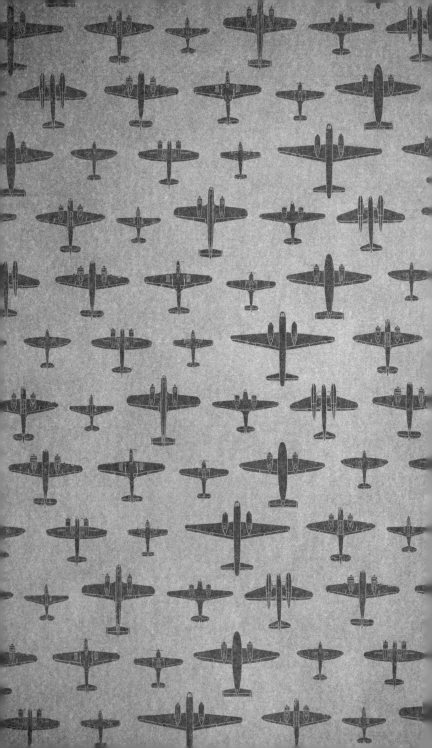